The Sky, the Stars,
the Wilderness

The Sky, the Stars, the Wilderness

RICK BASS

HOUGHTON MIFFLIN COMPANY

BOSTON · NEW YORK 1997

For information about permission to reproduce selections from
this book, write to Permissions, Houghton Mifflin Company,
215 Park Avenue South, New York, New York 10003.

Library of Congress Cataloging-in-Publication Data
Bass, Rick, date.
The sky, the stars, the wilderness / Rick Bass.
p.   cm.
ISBN 0-395-71758-2
I. Title.
PS3552.A82135S5   1997
813'.54 — dc21   97-24379
                                    CIP

"The Myths of Bears" was previously
published in the *Southern Review*.
"Where the Sea Used to Be" was
previously published in the *Paris Review*.

Printed in the United States of America

QUM 10 9 8 7 6 5 4 3 2 1

Printed on recycled paper

For Elizabeth, Mary Katherine, Lowry

ACKNOWLEDGMENTS

I am grateful to my editors, Camille Hykes, Harry Foster, and Dorothy Henderson, to my typist, Angi Young, to Melodie Wertelet, for the book's design, and to Russell Chatham, for the lovely painting. I am grateful to the editors of the *Southern Review* and the *Paris Review* for editing and publishing, respectively, "The Myths of Bears" and "Where the Sea Used to Be." I am also grateful to the late J. Frank Dobie, Dick Holland, Neal Durando, and the Southwest Texas Writers Collection for help with "The Myths of Bears" and to Jerry Scoville for help with "The Sky, the Stars, the Wilderness." The characters and stories in this collection came from the imagination and do not represent any persons or incidents known to me.

CONTENTS

The Myths
of Bears

"In all that hardness and cruelty there is a knowledge to be gained, a necessary knowledge, acquired in the only way it can be, from close familiarity with the creatures hunted. A knowledge of blood, of sinew and gut; of the structure of joint and muscle, the shape of the skull, the angularity, the sharpness or roundness of nose and ears and lips and teeth. There is passion in the hand that pulls the pelt and strokes the fur, confident that it knows as second nature all the hinges and recesses of the animal body. But however close that familiarity, something is always withheld; the life of the animal remains other and beyond, never completely yielding all that it is."

— John Haines, *The Stars, the Snow, the Fire*

I

TRAPPER IS SO OLD AND TIRED THAT EVERY AUGUST
he just sits in the sun in front of his cabin with his head
bowed, trying to gather up the last of it. A week of heat left,
and then each day after will be cooler. He sits with his arms
spread and tries to gather it all in, absorbing the vitamin D.
Everything is draining from him. He used to love winter
the most; now he tries only to stagger from August to August, crossing the months like steppingstones across a dangerous river.

Maybe the breadth of time he's spent in the woods
turned Trapper's mind: his need to be versatile, to change
with the seasons. Or maybe it's the absence of cities, towns,
or villages. It wasn't something, though, that human con-
tact could stave off in him, or else his wife would have kept
it at bay. He wants her back worse than he ever wanted a
pelt. Judith has been gone now almost a year.

She broke through the cabin's small window on a January night during the wolf moon when Trapper was having
one of his fits. At such times something wild enters him.
Trapper is as pale as a snow lion. Judith came from Tucson,
and was still brown ten years after she left. It was as though
in Arizona she'd stored a lifetime of sun.

Judith has curved feet, like flippers. She's six feet tall
(Trapper is five-nine), and her shoe size is thirteen. Judith
gets around in the snow well; the inward curve of her feet
makes it so she doesn't need snowshoes.

*

In Trapper's nighttime fits, he imagines that he is a wolf, and that the other wolves in his pack have suddenly turned against him and set upon him with their teeth; he's roused in bed to snarl and snap at everything in sight.

And then there are the daytime fits, when he imagines he has become someone else, in the manner of a snowshoe hare or ptarmigan, whose coat changes color with the seasons, and the deer and caribou, whose habits change; or the bear, who goes to sleep, falling down into that deep, silent place, beneath a dozen feet of snow, by January, where his brave heart beats once a minute — where everything's very, very slow . . .

When Trapper would get that way — *changed* — he would turn to Judith and begin speaking in the third person, as if neither he nor she were there.

His eyes wouldn't blink as he turned slowly to her to say, "Trapper says there is a storm coming," or, "Trapper says there are too many wolves in the woods," or, increasingly, "Trapper says he doesn't feel good."

Judith hated to leave him like that. When Trapper held his hands out in front of him they shook like leaves, and he was only thirty-five years old. Maybe his body would live forever, but his mind was going, and Judith was too smart to ride it to the end.

He had also begun to shake as he set his traps, fumbling with and bumping the hair triggers. Increasingly, he'd arrive home with crushed fingers.

"Trapper says he doesn't know what's happening," he'd say, and Judith's heart would flood away from her like loose water. She'd feel wicked about it, but she was changing, too — she could hear the distance calling her some nights, could see the northern lights whooshing and crackling so close as to seem just over the next ridge. She'd want to leave right then, right there. The northern lights, or something, were calling her name. Judith stayed as watchful in bed as a cat, never sleeping now as the lights sprayed green and red beams across the dark sky: she was waiting, waiting for one more wolf fit. When it finally came, she would be up and through that small glass window.

*

Judith cut herself breaking through it — Trapper had barred the door to keep trouble out, she knew, though as Trapper grew sicker Judith had begun to imagine it was to keep her in — and he'd been able to track her a ways, following her blood. Howling as he went, he sounded like a wolf in his sadness. But Trapper had had to stop to pull on his snowshoes at their place by the door and in this span of time Judith drew still farther away from him. She had the advantage of speed, and she knew where she was going — up and over that northern ridge — while Trapper had to pause, going from track to track, blood spot to blood spot. A heavy snow was beginning to fall through the trees as if trying to wash away the moon, and Judith ran for the ridge with her fifty-yard head start, and then it was a hundred yards; Judith was crying, and tears were freezing on her cheek, but she knew she was now about two hundred and fifty yards away from him. She could barely hear his howls.

She crossed a creek, soaking her boots up over the ankle; she gasped, and clambered to the other side, and started up the ridge. He was the only one who had ever really loved her — *her* — with her big crooked feet. Faintly she could still hear him.

Her feet were numb from the creek but she moved on, the quick falling snow covering her tracks.

When Judith got up to the ridge, his howls were gone. She considered howling once, to let him know she was — what? all right? not angry? sad? — but instead she turned and went down the ridge, catching herself on the trunks of the trees when she tripped.

Judith ran all night to stay warm, floundering, heading for the north. She knew he'd figure she was headed to a town.

It was true she'd be safe in a town, because Trapper would never enter one to look for her, but he might go so far as to hang around on the outskirts, like an old lobo skulking around a campfire.

Judith didn't miss the desert. Sometimes she did — in the spring usually — but right now she was thrilled to be half running, half swimming through rich deep snow. The sadness of her leaving him being transformed into the joy of freedom, and the joy of flight, too.

She imagined the sleeping bears beneath her. Her Uncle Harm had raised her in the desert outside Tucson and then she had taken up with Trapper when both she and Trapper were eighteen. Uncle Harm had been an old trapper and hunter and had tried to teach Trapper some things, but had not been entirely successful.

Another year and Judith and Trapper would've spent half their lives together.

It was delicious to swim through the snow.

The blizzard was a sign that she was meant to escape. A fool could have followed the swath of her tracks under normal conditions, but these weren't normal conditions. This was the first night of her life.

It wasn't about babies, or towns, or quilting bees. Domesticity. It wasn't about flowers, or about the desert in spring. It might not have even been about his snarling fits, or his lonely, flat-eyed, "Trapper says" fits.

It was about those red and green rods streaking through the sky.

He was gone, Judith knew. It would be a luxury to feel sad about it. He'd been gone for years. If he'd been a deer or moose, elk or caribou — if he'd been prey instead of predator — something would have noticed his odd demeanor, his slowing step — that *trembling* — and would have singled him out and brought him down.

Judith slept at the base of a giant fire-hollowed cedar for a short time before dawn. She took off her leather boots, socks, and leggings and tucked them between her body and clothes to dry. She half dozed with her hands around her naked feet, trying to warm and dry them. The cedar jungle where she had stopped offered shelter against much of the snow and wind; it was the place where the deer had taken refuge, too. They'd been living in the tangle of cedars for several weeks, ever since the storms had started, shedding their antlers and milling together for warmth. Great curved antlers lay scattered all around her; they were being covered quickly with skiffs of snow — the drifts weren't as deep, back in the cedars — and Judith could feel the deer watching her. She dreamed that she could feel the warmth of their breath as they moved slowly over to investigate. Her coat and pants were made of deer hide, deer that Trapper had shot for her to skin and sew into garments.

Judith slept as the deer circled and sniffed her and looked at one another in the deep night and waited out the storm.

The wolves would notice his odd gait, Judith dreamed. If Trapper tried to follow her too far in his condition — his *sleepwalking* — the wolves would get him.

Spring, even the hint of it, was still three months away.

She dreamed of Tucson, holding her cold toes in her hands: rubbing them in her sleep.

It was still snowing outside of the cedar jungle, when her shivering woke her in the early light. Judith considered whether she would forever after this night associate guilt with cold. She could see the tracks of deer around her where they had come in the night; she could see those places where they had stopped to sniff and identify her. They had touched her, she knew, with their noses: they had given her her identity.

It is not that he is a bad man, or that I am a bad woman, she thought. It's just that he is a predator, and I am prey. It

is the way of nature for our lives to be associated, even in-
tertwined, for a long while. But now if I am to survive, I
have to run. It has nothing to do with him. It *used* to; but
now, suddenly that I'm free, it doesn't.

It is so *sad,* she thought; but even as she was thinking
this, she was pulling on her damp socks, her damp boots
and leggings, and dusting the snow from her clothes and
rising stiffly, her legs as bow-legged from the cold as the
curve of her big sorrowful feet. She stared at the deer's delicate tracks.

He is gone, Judith told herself again. I am not running
from him anymore, I am running from his death.

Trapper is gone.

She looked up the next ridge, into the wind-and-north-
stunted alpine fir; a little farther north, she knew, there would
be tundra. She definitely did not want to leave the woods.

No, she remembered then, I am no longer running from
anything. I am running *to* something.

Her feet were hurting, which was good; the blood was
returning. Judith limped down a game trail. Snow continued to fall. Her long yellow hair shrouded her neck and
face and kept the snow out. It was too cold for the snow to
melt. Trapper used to brush her hair every night; brush it
and then wash it. Already she missed his broken-fingered
hands.

"Trapper is gone," she repeated out loud, as she trudged
up the trail. Later in the day, she would find a gaunt-ribbed
deer dying in the cedar jungle, starving, and she would
chase it a short distance — the deer falling and floundering,
crazy-legged, unable to go on — and she would kill it by
cutting its throat with her knife.

Judith drank the blood from the cut throat, but only after the deer was dead and its eyes were turning waxy blue,
its soul rising into the trees.

Then the liver, still hot; steam rising from it as she cut it
free. Then the blood that was sloshing around inside the

body cavity. Judith washed the blood from her face with handfuls of snow; skinned the deer quickly while it was still warm, before it could freeze, and cut the meat from the shoulders and hamstrings and wrapped it up in the congealed hide. Tied it to her back.

Judith felt the woods wrapping her, taking care of her in her sorrow, and she thanked the woods every step of the way for giving her a deer. She felt *embraced*. Judith knew this was how her Uncle Harm — the one who'd taught Trapper certain things, though not everything — used to feel, because he'd talked about it often, back in Arizona.

Deer stood aside, too cold to run, and watched her pass.

*

Judith felt badly: not knowing why she was moving, only that she must. Grizzlies will travel thirty miles in a night, she knew, to get to a good acorn crop. Deer and elk will leave a mountain, will come down off the highest peak and into the river bottoms in advance of a storm, in only a matter of hours. But Judith was not entirely sure why she was traveling, and why she was moving north, into the winter, rather than away from it.

It had been a hundred and six degrees on the day she was born. But she'd gotten used to the cold. It wasn't that different from the heat. Both were things that got your attention.

Maybe it was as simple as the feeling that if she went south, it would be like running away; but if she went north, it would just be running.

*

Trapper hunted her for four days and nights, making concentric circles around his cabin, trying to pick up her sign: making the circles larger and larger; calling her name and crying and howling. Chasing the game off: ruining his season.

Betrayed; abandoned. He'd thought she was *tame*. He'd not understood she was the wildest, most fluttering thing in the woods.

He thinks, Next time when I get her back, I will keep her tied up even tighter. I will tie her with rawhide to a stake in the front yard.

He thinks, She didn't love me enough. Maybe she even hated me. But what about all those good times in Tucson? And up here?

I will make her love me more, he thinks, wandering his woods, casting for scent, trembling, like an old dog. He hunts for her harder than he ever hunted for any grizzly or wolf, fisher or marten. He abandons his traps, forgets where he's hung them.

Martens dangle from the trunks of trees, a rear leg snapped, broken by the snap of the trap's jaws. At first the martens scramble and chatter to get free, but over time their movements become slower. They hang like small shawls against the tree trunks, snow catching on their fur, and the traps, rusting . . .

If Judith had heard Trapper cry like a child she probably would have gone back to him and stayed until he got better, or didn't. But some instinct told her to go all the way up to the edge of the forest: to winter away from him in a place where she could not be lured back.

Maybe in the spring, Judith thought, she'd ease back and spy on his cabin. See if he had made it or not. See if he'd survived or if he was bones.

Forty, fifty, fifty-five below. She can't build a fire, or he'll find her. She left in such a hurry. She builds a snow cave in the cedar jungles; makes a coat of her deer hide, but still she's cold, even with two coats. She doesn't dare build a fire. Even mind-sick, Trapper can smell smoke at a hundred miles.

Such is her fear, and the word beyond fear: *longing*.

*

Trapper sleeps with the window open — the one she crashed through — to punish himself for letting her escape. He knows she's not building fires. He'd smell them. If he could just find where she is, he could begin setting traps for her, but he has no idea whether she is east or west or north or south of him. He feels trapped by his ignorance, and thrashes around on his bed at night and moans and howls. His trap-cracked fingers surge with pain; they've been frostbitten so many times that each new time they freeze, he's sure he'll lose them, that this time the blood won't return, and what good is a trapper without fingers, without hands? He'd be no better than a bear, with nothing but paws.

Trapper remembers the big grizzly he killed down in the Gila desert, back in the nineties. Its tracks were thirteen inches by eleven inches — the bear's feet as long as Judith's, but so very much wider — and Trapper remembers how the bear dragged Trapper's chain and trap twelve miles up into the mountains, and into a cave. Trapper had nailed the trap and chain to a twelve-foot timber, and he followed the swath the bear made as he fled. October. Buzzards shadowed the bear, knowing what was coming. It was easy for Trapper to follow the bear at a dead run, as there were the birds to look to. The trail itself was like the wake of a canoe. Trapper has never owned a horse: he despises and distrusts anything stronger than he is.

As Trapper's shakes set in, Judith grew that way: stronger than he was. He still had his strength, but when he was trembling, it was of little use; he'd drop things. He'd have to ask her for help. The glimmer of reasoning that this might have frightened her as badly as it frightened him glows in his mind, and then fades. He's remembering this bear in the Gila.

You must tie a drag to the trap for them to run with, one which will only slow them down. If you tie the chain too tight, with no hope of escape, the bear or wolf will chew its damn *leg* off, to get away.

This Gila River grizzly holed up in a cave. It was a smart bastard. It ambushed Trapper, trap and chain and log and all. Wrapped Trapper up as best as it could. Biting at Trapper's face and neck. The only thing that saved Trapper was the fact that the bear's teeth had been broken by the huge steel trap: he'd tried to bite it off. Still, the bear raked Trapper's back with his terrible claws. The first bear that ever got in close with Trapper; the first one he ever wrapped up with. Trapper was nineteen. Trapper grabbed the bear's big tongue the way he'd been told and twisted like hell; the bear released his grip, and Trapper pulled his big knife free and stuck it up under the ribs, again and again, probing for the heart. Found it.

Bright red blood and froth and bits of tooth all over his face. He had to sleep on his stomach for three months. He remembers how Judith would lick the wounds; and then, when they healed, how she would lick the scars. They were living on her Uncle Harm's ranch, in an adobe by the Salt River. White-winged doves cooing all the time. The mornings were cool; everything seemed new.

Nineteen!

He didn't know if his seed was bad or if she was barren. Nothing ever happened, and he's not sure, as he trembles now, ancient at thirty-five, that that was a bad thing.

Candlelight washes across his crooked face. He can't believe he's alone.

*

In February it warmed to fifteen below. It had been so cold that Judith's head hurt: she grew a little crazy, afraid to sleep for fear that her head would split the way the dry fir trees had been every January night. She couldn't move around, couldn't walk through the woods with her ugly feet unless it was snowing hard; she couldn't risk leaving tracks.

Judith figured she was about twenty-five miles north of him. She could sense by the stillness in the woods — the utter emptiness and newness and peace — that he had no idea where she was hiding.

But he would find out. He would sense that peace — he would feel her feeling it — and he would be drawn toward it. She would have to be ready to move again, and quickly.

She wanted to get away, but not too far away.

There were nights when she felt he was still tied to her: she knew he was out tracking her. Strangely, she felt *loved*.

But it felt fine to be alone, and to be free of his air. It wasn't bad air that he breathed in and out; it was just *his*.

When it began to snow, she would rise and go for walks in the woods, walking through the heaviest snowstorms. She'd found a winter-killed moose and made a robe of that, to add to her other coats. She wore all of them when she walked, and when she got lost and could not find her way back to her snow cave, as frequently happened, she'd build a new one. She was following a ridge above a river bottom over into the next valley. It was a country Trapper had never worked before, and sometimes Judith would catch herself with the ludicrous thought that she would have to tell him about it when she got back.

Remember, Judith told herself, *he is gone*.

She was pretty sure he was gone.

Her hair was wild and dirty, turning darker, from yellow blond to dirty blond, which troubled her. But it wasn't enough to turn back for: the simple touch of his busted-up hands, brushing and washing her hair, and a warm fire.

A wolverine confronted her one day, ran scampering around her snow cave, raising his hind leg and pissing all around it, a vile scent that reminded her of maggots. He stuck his snarling face into her cave and Judith screamed and jabbed her knife at him, cutting his nose, and the wolverine ran away, lunging across the snow like a man with a broken back, squalling and leaving a trail of blood but looking over his shoulder at her as if to say, "I'll be back."

Judith cut a heavy walking stick and lashed the sharpest deer antlers she could find to the end of it. She never went anywhere without it, and had nightmares about the wolverine until she found him dead in March, where wolves had killed him.

The meat of the wolverine had been too mean and vile for the wolves to eat; they'd eaten only his entrails. Ravens led her to his carcass. It pleased Judith to think of the wolves eating his guts. But she moved on, because he'd marked her cave as his territory, and the woods were spoiled.

She kept moving north whenever it snowed, moving from one pocket of stillness and peace to the next. It was exactly as if she had an injury, and had to let the muscle and bone knit and regather strength. It took time.

In February, Trapper had abandoned his cabin and gone south looking for her. By the first week he knew she could be dead and under five or six feet of snow — he might not find her skeleton for ten or twenty years, or ever — but he pushed on, casting for scent. He knew she would cross at least one divide, and possibly two. The way she had hit that window, he knew she was terrified of something.

It was the first time in eighteen years that he hadn't spent a winter trapping; it felt good. He stood by his fire each night, the trembling having spread from his hands to his shoulders and legs. He was alone, and he acknowledged this — there was something wrong with him, something which time would not fix — but he felt *good.*

He'd piss on his campfire each night to let the wolves know he was in the woods. He heard their howls, the whole of the woods echoing with their sound. Trapper knew that in winter they were all only two days away from starving.

He worked a hundred miles south in a week, and then

fifty miles east of that line, coming back across it, and fifty miles west.

"Sombofambitch," he said in March, when he finally felt the peace, and could acknowledge its presence. He was having trouble with his speech. "She has gonb Norf . . . Norf . . . Norf." His heart was fluttering, and his legs, when they trembled, felt like a colt's.

He was back at his cabin padding traps with hides, as he didn't want her to have an ankle broken. He would set them in the spring.

The scent, or feel, of her peace reminded him of the northern lights. No one else he knew ever claimed they could hear them, but he could: the sound was faint to be sure, but clearly there, and it was like strips of thin metal delicately chiming. Trapper believed in angels and a God, though he had never seen either, and believed without doubt that the red and green of the northern lights showed where angels had been: just a day's passage ahead of him, or two at most.

Trapper started north with a hundred pounds of traps slung over his shoulder. He hadn't used sled dogs in five years, because the wolves always killed them, and he was tired of the heartache of losing them.

Aiming north and west, he figured she'd head for the ocean — women love oceans, he thought, and men love forests.

He came near her on that trip, missing her by less than a mile. Judith was sitting on the bluff looking out over the western river bottom when she felt his presence in the woods and then, an hour later, saw him go walking below her, all those heavy chains thrown across his shoulder: his steps with the snowshoes looking big and sloppy.

She watched him cross the frozen river with his traps. She couldn't see his face or even his beard, and certainly not his strange blue eyes, which turned almost violet in late winter, as if in anticipation, perhaps, of spring.

She could make out his wide back, the heavy robes he was wearing, and his clumsy steps. She watched as if it were her wedding day; she felt that much love for him, and that much relief that he was missing her. He stopped often to look at tracks in the river bottom, but they were not her tracks.

In Arizona, Trapper had fried everything in lion grease. Pancakes, sausage, elk steaks, or fish — it all sizzled in the sweet fat of the mountain lions he killed. Old folks said that it would go to his brain and give him the trembles later in life, and maybe it did, but watching him move across the river bottom — trembling, though still somehow in possession of his strength — Judith doesn't think that's what did it.

She thinks it is the force of God blowing through the trees that makes him shake. He has chased things so hard and for so long that he has gotten cut off. He's gotten lost, or dead-ended, or trapped. Or something.

Anyway, he didn't look ready to die. He looked like he was holding steady.

Judith watched Trapper cross the river: heading all the way to the coast, she suspected — salmon, boats, fishing villages — just to look for her.

It made her feel good in a way she hadn't felt in a long while.

Trapper moved slowly. Judith stayed behind a tree. He was hundreds of feet below her, and half a mile off. Once he turned and looked back up the bluff, right at her. Tears began to roll down Judith's cheeks, freezing before they fell, as she felt all of her precious space shattering in his gaze, his *discovery*, but he was looking right through her. Trapper turned away again.

Immediate relief became joy, but then Judith felt an echo of sadness, like a stone dropped, clacking to the bottom of a nearly dry well on a hot day.

Trapper made his way across the mile-wide river. He

didn't have long to get to the coast and back before the breakup of the ice left him stranded — the river would surge in a month or six weeks with jagged icebergs, cracking and booming, frothing with dead moose and bear bobbing in its torrent, young foolish animals who'd tried to cross it . . . It occurred to Judith that maybe Trapper wasn't coming back.

He still had not come straight north. She believed that when he did not find her on the coast, he would come back and try the forest — the last place he would have suspected her to be. It was a miracle that he had not seen her when he'd looked back up the bluff in her direction. Judith had held her breath to keep from breathing out smoke-vapor, and hadn't *blinked* — just those round, crystal, frozen tears leaking from her. Judith had seen Trapper spot live animals hidden in the forest at distances greater than half a mile. Despite the beauty of his violet eyes, he was color-blind; he saw a monochromatic version of the world, grainy blacks and whites of tone. Winter didn't bother him, because it was how he always saw the world — and animals that relied on the tones of camouflage were helpless, revealed bluntly, nakedly, before his gaze.

After Trapper was gone, Judith felt sorrow and fear, but then the fear left and joy returned. She wished him well on his journey and worried for him, but reasoned that any time spent trembling in the woods was infinitely preferable to time spent trembling on a bed in a cabin or — worse — in a town.

Judith imagined that the space to the north of her, all the way to the North Pole, was hers — her *own* space.

She could not wait for spring, when color would fill that space, and her world would burst with life.

*

They had left Arizona when the first silver and copper mines were going in and cattle were sweeping across the desert and fouling the brief rivers. There had been trout a foot and a half long in the Santa Cruz River, and steamships had cruised up and down it — but five years after the cattle showed up, the rivers had turned to silt plains, and there weren't enough wolves to turn the cattle back. Trapper regretted that he had helped see to that.

He had never poisoned wolves the way the ranchers did. He trapped them instead, and then hit them in the head with a club to keep from ruining the pelt.

Judith's Uncle Harm was the one who had taught him how to trap. Judith has tried to imagine Trapper being anything else in life — a miner, or a schoolteacher — but can't see it. She takes this to mean that if he had not met up with Uncle Harm and herself, Trapper would be dead. Invisible.

She takes this to mean, indirectly, that she saved his life. If he had not fallen in hot love with her, he would never have learned to trap.

Uncle Harm was seventy-seven and failing when Trapper showed up. He still hunted and trapped, but Uncle Harm was hunting with dogs mostly by that time, and no longer tried to get physically involved with his prey.

When he'd been younger, Trapper's age, Uncle Harm had hunted the way Trapper did — on foot, stalking and laying traps, shooting from ambush, and taking on the animals in his traps with only a knife or a club. Uncle Harm was the first white man to perfect the old Yaqui trick of hunting down and engaging a grizzly — getting it to charge — and then swatting its wrists with an iron bar, breaking them, thereby evening the odds considerably; dodging the crippled bear's jaws and killing it with a knife or lance after that.

The worst Uncle Harm ever got it was from a Mexican grizzly down in Chihuahua. The grizzly was so big that it simply pulled free of the giant trap, leaving behind part of its foot and two huge claws.

Whenever Uncle Harm spoke of this he always took

care to mention how the flesh-end nerves of the freshly pulled claws were still red with life, glowing in the trap.

The tracks of the escaped bear were plain, and Uncle Harm, a young man of thirty-three at the time, followed them easily and quickly. At a sharp bend of the trail he found what he wanted. The hurt grizzly had backtracked to the bend to wait.

There was no time to lift his club or his knife. The bear knocked Uncle Harm down with one swat, breaking his collarbone, and then bit him on the skull — Judith had heard Uncle Harm preach that the human skull is irresistible to grizzlies, that they like to puncture it like a ring-tailed cat popping eggs — and then when the bear heard Uncle Harm's skull pop he moved his attentions to Uncle Harm's shoulders and began ripping them and chewing.

Uncle Harm was dying fast, and he knew his only chance was to play dead, which he was having no trouble doing. He shut his eyes while the grizzly picked him up and dragged him back and forth across the manzanita, smearing the brush with his blood. Still Uncle Harm played dead, trying to outlast the grizzly's rage.

The grizzly finally dropped him and ran off, only to return to shake him again so hard that it almost broke Uncle Harm's neck. The grizzly bit him in the face, then stood over Uncle Harm before nosing him, as if trying to bring his victim back to life so he could kill him again. The bear leaned down and snorted in Uncle Harm's ear, trying to make him jump, but Uncle Harm remained dead.

Uncle Harm heard the bear limp off after that, and consciousness left him.

When he awoke it was night. He crawled back down the creek to a small spring. Another wolf hunter found him the next day. They sewed him up with veterinary supplies, "but my looks," Uncle Harm would always say, motioning to his terrible, grinning face, "were never thereafter complimentary."

Trapper loved the old man: loved him deeply. Sometimes Judith thinks Trapper should have married Uncle Harm instead of her. He loved to be with the old man. Uncle Harm fried all his food in lion grease too, though he never got the shakes. When Harm got really old and had to resort to chasing animals with dogs rather than on foot, he would circle around the desert on his mule with a gramophone lifted to his old near-deaf ears, trying to pick up the sound and direction of his dogs' squalls as they battled a bear or a lion. He insisted on going out on his own — wouldn't share his territory, the Galliero Mountains, with anyone, not even Trapper — and when he got older still, there were days when Trapper and Judith didn't know if he'd make it back. At such times, they would go out looking for him.

Sometimes they would find him unscathed — he'd have gotten tired and stopped to camp by a creek on his way in, with a grizzly hide and the quartered carcass packed across his mule, his dogs panting in the shade, all scratched and cut up from the fight — Uncle Harm looking five or ten years younger every time he killed something. But there were other times, sad times, when they'd go out and find Uncle Harm, made loopy from dehydration, spinning in circles on his back on the desert floor, staring crazily up at the great white autumn clouds while his dogs stood around him in a confused circle, wanting to step in and lick him but unable to move in among his spinning arms and legs; the saddled mule would be off in the shade chewing saltbush, unconcerned, with no grizzly or lion pelt across its saddle. Uncle Harm looked a hundred years old on such days, and wild-eyed, too, and with his canteen stone-empty . . .

Judith and Trapper would gather him up, lift him onto his fool mule, give him water, and put his hat back on him to shield him from the sun. They would walk back home: a whole day's hunting ruined for Trapper, but he didn't care. Back then Trapper could take it or leave it. Uncle Harm's facial scars glowed pale blue whenever he had a heat stroke.

There was a muddy creek behind their adobe house, and they'd float him in that until he returned to himself.

By nightfall, when the coyotes were singing, Harm would be better; he'd have crawled out from the creek and gone to his little house (Trapper and Judith lived in the big house) and there he would change into his white linen evening suit. He'd fix a cup of piñon tea and go sit on his porch and listen to the night. He'd tell Trapper and Judith trapping stories, and secrets, and in the morning, though there would be new scars and stretchmarks upon his heart, he would be ready to go out and kill again.

He kept going. Judith thought it was half-monstrous and half-heroic — it was just the kind of thing a man would like and admire — the way Uncle Harm ruined himself. He kept driving, mindless, *pursuing*. It makes her sad to realize that the times she loved Trapper most were when he was hunting the least. It makes her feel guilty, too, because when Trapper was not hunting he was paying attention to her, and loving her. Does this mean she can't love Trapper for what he is, but rather, only for what he can give her?

Nobody could be that selfish, she thinks. It's simply a matter of where he puts his heart. It's very simple, Judith thinks. He puts his heart in the woods, or he puts it in the palm of her hand. His heart clenches hers as though they are two elk with their noble antlers linked, if only by accident, in combat.

Back before Harm had broken off the gramophone horn to take with him, Judith would stay in bed with Trapper all through the hot part of the day, the sweet middle, falling in and out of sleep, *languishing*, rousing only to put a new record on the gramophone: both of them abed in the cool shade of love, never suspecting that in a few short years the desert would be gone. Shitting cattle would scour it, and water-robbing mesquite would grow out of their manure, muffins cast like steppingstones across the land, and with that the rarest and wildest creatures would leave, vanishing.

The last music Judith heard, other than the howls of wolves, was in 1904. She listens for the northern lights that Trapper says he can hear, but still she hears nothing: though even the sound of nothing, with enough space around her, is pleasant and sweet. Not as good as the sound of running water, which she knows will be coming, but in winter the sound of nothing is just right. The howls of wolves reassure, and comfort her: as though a deal has been struck whereby they will take sadness from her heart and assume it for themselves.

Judith builds a tiny cabin out of wind-felled timbers, stretches her hide over it for a roof; packs it with snow.

Trapper didn't look sick, she thinks. Maybe he has gotten better without me.

This inspires in her the desire to capture him and see if it is so. Judith's not sure she *wants* him to be better off without her.

*

It isn't about children, Judith tells herself. She remembers the old woman they met in Yellowknife who introduced herself as having had thirteen children by her first husband, but her new husband, Art, "his seed is bad."

Judith knows women with children who've run, and she knows women without children, such as herself, who have also run.

Uncle Harm trapped or killed almost everything in Arizona and then died in 1909 at the age of ninety-one. He'd taken to shooting cows when there was nothing else around; dropping them like buffalo, fifteen and twenty at a time, and then hiding out and waiting for the coyotes and the last few lobos to come skulking in. It was easier to find him, once he started shooting the cows. Buzzards would spiral above wherever he'd made his stand.

His dogs were by his side, guarding him, the day that

Trapper and Judith found him for the last time. Wizened, Uncle Harm had already been gone about half a day, headed toward wherever he was going beyond this life. His gramophone horn was curled up tightly in his little fist and Judith took it from him gently. After they'd buried him she tried to hook it back up and play it, but it wouldn't work, not even after they cleaned all the dust and grit out of it.

They had to bury him off in the desert so he wouldn't foul the spring. Piled rocks up on his grave forming a cairn, but still the remaining coyotes and wolves came and gathered around it and howled every night for a month. The summer rains came, and they could see where a few grizzlies had appeared from hiding and circled the cairn as if having to see for themselves that yes, it was true, they were safe now. Ravens circled the cairn for weeks, diving and spiraling. Damnedest thing either of them had ever seen, with the exception of Uncle Harm himself.

They sold his dogs to a cattle rancher, opened all the doors and windows of the adobe houses to let the desert enter, and went up through the Rockies in the spring. But the grizzlies and wolves and Indians had vanished there, too, so they kept going farther north.

Trapper and Judith didn't reach the Yukon until fall.

When they started hearing wolves, they felt better. As if they had come home; as if what mattered lay south or north of their country, but not in between.

2

It's Trapper's aim to catch wolves and martens and wolverines on his trip to the coast, and pull the hides behind him on a sled, arriving at the coast a rich man and trading for gold, for groceries. Coffee from Africa and sugar from the tropics, to maybe keep Judith happy this time. Maybe while she's staked out in the yard he will bake her things with sugar in them. Maybe she would enjoy his new riches so much that he wouldn't even have to keep her staked, at least not all the time.

She's lost her mind, Trapper muses, moving through the woods, shaking and stutter-stepping. She hit that window like a bat out of hell. It was like something old Harm might have done.

Big smoked salmon, and new traps, new ammunition, too — lead and gun powder. And jewelry: he'll trap her with gold jewelry, he thinks; he'll string it all through the woods and then set snares, or hide up in a tree, so that when she reaches for the glittering-with-sun necklace he can catch her wrist in a wire noose, and he'll have her, again. The mistake last time was that he didn't hold her tight enough, that he gave her too much rein . . .

He'll build smaller windows.

More leg-hold traps: more tobacco. Fuck horses! He'll pull it all home on a sled himself, the way he's always done. Fuck dogs! Whiny crybabies anyway, always wanting to rest. Always getting eaten by wolves. His beard and eyebrows are shining dull whitish-blue with frost — it's thirty below — and he howls.

The wolves that have been following him at a distance draw closer, knowing they are safe when a fit wells up from within him; at such times they know that he is not a man, but rather is one of them. They seem to believe he would be loath to kill one of his own kind — a brother, a sister.

It's so lonely without her.

What if she's not even up here any more? What if she's back in Arizona at this very moment? He's ashamed that his heart is a weak little muscle, incapable of matching the great strength of the chest in which it is housed. Can it be true that he is as weak in heart and mind and soul as Harm was in body? Can it be that he might have an animal's soul trapped within his body? Maybe that's why trapping never bothered him.

Delicate ladylike weasels with their front leg bent sideways and shattered in the trap quiver and look at him in fright as he approaches; they grasp the jaws of the big trap with the slender fingers of their uninjured paw. Already the beautiful shawl they wear does not belong to them . . .

A man can be a horrible thing. Trapper sits on a log and howls and weeps, but there seems to be no escape. And he does not know where he wants to escape *to*.

He hears a movement in the brush and snow behind him. He grabs his rifle and turns and raises it and sees a pale silver wolf running away from him. Trapper fires and sends the wolf tumbling, but he's only wounded it; the wolf is back up and running again. There are other wolves with it, and so he will not go into the brush after it, though the blood trail tempts him.

It's not his fault that Judith got away, part of him tells himself, when he's shaking, when he's trying to become whatever it is his body's trying to make him become, even if only fodder for worms; but the other part of him, the stronger part, says, "She was in your dominion, and you had control of her, and you lost her."

For thirty miles slogging through snow he thinks of words like "dominion" and replays every day of their life together, putting the days together like tracks, but he's puzzled, can find no sign of error, no proof of her unhappiness with him.

He's got four wolf pelts, six foxes, a dozen weasels, a coyote, and a wolverine on his sled, his stone boat, which he drags through the forest. He tries to think like the animals, and yet at the same time tries to keep his wits about him and keep from plunging off the cliff of human reason and into some abyss where he believes that man, having failed at something, descends to a level equal with the animals.

Loopy with fatigue, Trapper snaps off the branches of winter-thin willows along a creek and weaves them into a crown, and continues on his way, carrying his traps with him as he goes.

*

On the coast, Trapper asks around, speaking all three languages — Yúpik, French, and English — awkwardly: the damn woods having swallowed his tongue. But no one's seen her.

The men and women cluck their tongues. One old woman laughs at him, and says to Trapper in Yúpik, "If you lived here she would be easy to trap, for she would have nowhere to run to but the sea."

He stays a night, buys sex from a villager for one wolf pelt — an outrageous price — and makes his trades the next day, and turns and heads back across the tundra, back to the woods, with another storm coming in behind him from off the Arctic Ocean. He'll trap on the way home too, though he must be careful and hurry, or he'll run out of snow in places and ruin his sled pulling it across the bare rocks.

And then there's the river. Trapper can't swim. He can do all manner of things, spectacular things, with his body, if not his mind, but he's so freighted with muscle that whenever he gets in water he goes straight to the bottom. Like a rock.

Trapper moves through the woods herking and jerking, pulling his load, trying, with his mind alone, to trick his central nervous system into not disintegrating further; into not acknowledging that disintegration. He notices that he's trying to tie his knots backward, and it scares him.

To keep his mind off how far this nonsense can go, he concentrates on bears. He imagines how the woods are full of sleeping bears, all denned up beneath him, six feet beneath his snowshoes and curled, waiting to come to life. He thinks of bears, and goes over the facts versus the myths.

Bears do *not* suck their paws in hibernation. They merely sleep with their paws pressed up against their faces. The Indians in southern British Columbia maintained that a grizzly sighting a lone man in the forest would stand up and hold out one paw toward the man, even if seen or scented at a distance, to try and tell if the man was *skookum* — brave.

What's it going to be like to be dead, Trapper catches himself wondering. He views the trembling as accelerated old age, or fatigue, but now he remembers Uncle Harm spinning in the desert on his back, looking up at those clouds.

The thing was, Uncle Harm always got better. They'd lie him down in that cool water, and then later in the evening they'd see him come stepping out of the Arizona darkness in that glowing white linen suit. They'd smell his piñon tea. He'd sit down on their porch and tell them stories: true stories, amazing things that seemed capable of holding even death at bay.

The bear up near Prescott that kept raiding Uncle Harm's family's garden when Harm was a boy. Harm and his friend Dobie, fourteen years old, waiting up and watching in the moonlight as the silver-tipped grizzly came ambling into the garden and began swatting down the corn. July night thunder, monsoons walking across the far horizon, illuminated by heat lightning. A feeling, with all that thunder coming, Uncle Harm said, that you had to *kill* something.

With lanterns and rifles, Harm and Dobie would start yelling and sic their dogs on the great bear and head out for the garden, running hard: half-crazy and half-brave, even then. (Dobie died young.)

The bear would gather up all the corn it could carry, holding it under one arm, and run. A grizzly can hit speeds of up to forty miles an hour, and runs as strong going up a hill as down, due to the excessive piston musculature of its hind legs. Certainly even on three legs the grizzly could outrun two boys and their pissant dogs. The boys tracked him more by following the spilled ears of corn than with the aid of their cowardly pet dogs, but could never catch up with the grizzly, could never bring it to bay.

The grizzly kept coming back every night. Sometimes the boys heard him; other times they slept through his raids.

Finally one night Harm and Dobie stole a real dog, an Airedale that belonged to a friend of Dobie's father. The neighbor lived a half-mile away. They muzzled the dog so the owner wouldn't wake up in the night and hear his dog off on a bear trail, alone, and they tied double leashes to him so that he couldn't get away. Tied the other ends around their waists.

Lay down on the dark porch in ambush and waited. August, now, and the corn beginning to dry up. They could feel something was nearing an end.

"Tonight we get him," Dobie whispered.

After midnight they heard the bear in the corn again, and they waited, letting him fill his belly so he'd be easier to chase. There was a wind in their faces, and the Airedale, with cloth wrapped around his muzzle, whined softly, but the breeze carried his sounds away from the bear. Lightning storms rippled across the plateaus to the south.

When the bear stood and began knocking down roasting ears to take with him, Harm and Dobie turned the Airedale loose, and were snatched off the porch and out into the garden after him.

Uncle Harm said they each broke an arm; that the Airedale took them seven miles up into the mountains, that he would not stop, and that Dobie split his chin on a rock.

Still, the Airedale carried them on: across tiny mountain creeks, farther up into the mountains. They'd spy a dropped ear of corn every now and then. Sometimes they'd see the silver bear disappearing over a ridge: running hard on all fours now, with the Airedale hard after him. Dobie had dropped his lantern and rifle when he split his chin, then had been whisked on, snatched along by the Airedale's mad rage. The lantern had started a small fire where he dropped it, and then, climbing farther up the mountain, the Airedale jerked Harm off his feet, and Harm lost his lantern as well; then was dragged along.

As they neared the top of the mountain, they could see the two small fires burning in the piñon below them. At the top of the mountain, with the Airedale close to baying the bear, the Airedale summoned a last charge and broke free of his harness, which probably saved the boys, allowing Harm to continue on his way to becoming an old man, and Dobie to live another two years.

The Airedale engaged the grizzly up against the mouth of a cave. The dog must have known it couldn't *bite* the bear, with his muzzle still bound up in the tight-knotted muzzle, but such was his fury that he flew at the bear anyway.

Harm and Dobie crested the mountain, gasping. They saw the bear swat the Airedale through the air, the dog limp even as he flew away. The bear was standing at the mouth of a penned-up cave. Four or five pigs were grunting and squealing behind him in the cave; there were corn husks everywhere, as the bear had been feeding the pigs, fattening them up.

The bear squinted and raised his paw slowly, still standing, and held it out toward the boys as if trying to feel their heat: holding it the way a man next to a campfire might turn his palms to the flames to warm them.

Harm, with his rifle, was shaking so badly he couldn't begin to lift it; it was all he could do to keep from dropping it.

The bear didn't run. It kept standing there, holding its paw out toward the boys and sniffing the night-storm air. Uncle Harm said that both boys had the feeling — unspoken between them at the time, but passing through the air like an electrical current — that that bear wanted to catch them alive and put them in that pen with the pigs, and fatten *them* up.

They ran down the mountain stumbling and bleeding, with lightning booming all around them, and never told anyone where the Airedale had gone. Told their parents they'd gotten in a fight, is how they busted each other up.

The storm put out their fire, though for forty years, Harm said, you could see where they'd been: and the bear never came back to the garden.

"Cave's still up there," Harm had told Trapper. "Pig skeletons, too. And dog skeleton. Never did find a bear skeleton on that mountain. Could have been that bear was God."

"Could be too that we're all little pigs that the real God's got penned up on this earth," Harm said, and then laughed.

"I want to know what happened to Dobie," Judith had said.

Harm laughed. "Drowned," he said. He looked at Trapper and laughed again, his old face stretching and then falling slack, stretching and falling slack. "You and him resemble each other in the face," he said, meaning Dobie. He reached out and tousled Trapper's wild hair.

*

He finds one stretch of woods that's *rampant* with game. He knows he shouldn't linger — he knows he should get on back to the river, and across — but he cannot help himself. He camps for a week and takes not one, but two, wolverines — the second one being the mate of the first, who kept coming around after the first one was taken — and he traps foxes, too.

And wolves: always, wolves.

He pushes on again, but he's running late. The snow's melting, and freezing again at night. It's rough and chopped up; roots and boulders are emerging. Trapper slips, falls often. Sometimes he can't get up and has to struggle to reach for his sled, pulling a bloody wolf or fox hide from the stack to drape it across himself for warmth as night falls. The hide itself freezes during the night, fitting itself to Trapper's shape. He hears wolves howl and has to bite his cheeks to keep from joining in — they'd come investigate, otherwise, and then his dreams might come true: the pack swarming him, casting judgment for all the pack members, the brotherhood that he's killed — all the days of life he's robbed.

Trapper knows there aren't any *proven* stories of wolves killing a white man. Uncle Harm's told him that for some reason they used to eat the hell out of Frenchmen, Eskimos, and Russians, but that's no consolation as he quivers in the night, caught in the form-fitting frozen fox hide.

Oh, for a wife or a dog!

3

The river ice changes color in the last days of March, from white to gray, and from gray to thin blue, and Judith sits on the bluff and watches this. She listens to the ice groan and creak as it strains to move again. She listens to the wolves howling. It is harder for them to hunt once winter is gone. In winter they can chase hoofed animals, the weak ones, out onto the frozen lakes and ponds.

Poor wolves, she thinks, watching the woods for Trapper's return. The days are warm enough now that she doesn't need fires, but finally, she builds them along the bluff, and throws wet duff on them to make them smoke.

It's terrible without the thought of him out there chasing her, hunting her. It's horrible. There's too much space.

The river thaws first into ice floes that crash against each other, and then into fast blue water.

Still he does not appear.

She remembers how Trapper gathered her urine once a month to use it with his traps; she remembers how, that one time each month, the wolves would gather around their cabin and howl for a night or two, which excited Trapper terribly, made him pace the tiny cabin all night.

He'd shout into the dark, and sometimes shoot his rifle: taking a bead on the great full grinning moon and then shouting, in the rifle's echo-roar, when the moon did not fall, and when the wolves did not stop howling.

Maybe her womb was barren, or maybe his seed was bad. Or maybe both. Or maybe it was like the wolf and the wolverine, who were not meant to mix; like the bear and the badger.

She considers children. Remembers a man in Arizona whose son was killed by a bear, and who hunted that bear down, killed it, skinned it, and then slept on that hide every night for the rest of his life — another sixty-three years of falling asleep — or not — in the warmth of the killer's thick fur.

Thinking these things, Judith grows fond of her times with Trapper, and then one day, he appears. A white-haired crooked-standing figure on the far side of the river. It's him, with about a thousand pelts on his sled.

Judith turns and runs: into the woods, leaping logs like a deer. She doesn't *want* to go back to the past, or back to the lovesick days in Arizona with roast suckling goat and chimichurri sauce for breakfast, margaritas, and those doves cooing while they went back to bed and made love: Harm, not Trapper, off in the desert.

It feels wonderful to be running again.

Trapper has been seeing the smoke from her fires for days now; it's what turned him around. He's been walking in circles, lost for the first time in his life, just a few miles from the river. He knows what is happening to him. He's busted open the skulls of a million animals, gathering their brains to use for tanning their own hides, and he's compared the highly ridged convolutions of a bear's brains with the smoother, duller loops and folds of a marten, or the blankness of a boar-musky raging wolverine's brain — and Trapper can feel a certain silliness, a kind of numbness, like a skullcap, settling over the top of his own mind.

The loops of his brain-folds are losing their edges.

Maybe it was the lion grease. Or loneliness.

He's been walking in circles, setting traps that don't catch anything. Sometimes he steps in his own traps — by some miracle avoiding the forty-five-pound bear traps that would cut his legs off — but even when the traps clap shut on his ankle or his hand, he doesn't really *feel* it.

But the smoke: he still knew enough to go to the smoke. He still had the instinct, if not the knowledge, that somehow she could save him.

He'd stake her out yet. His arms are wizened, slack-muscled, and he stares at them, then squints across the river. She's probably stronger than he is now, he thinks. He'll have to do it with cunning.

He feels the loops unfolding. Thinks of how wolves pull the slick entrails out first and gulp them down, sometimes while the animal is still alive.

Trapper doesn't blink. He can't feel anything. A million hardnesses are beginning to crash down upon him, and all he can think is, I want a million and one.

4

It was thought by the savages of the north, Trapper knows, that bears were half god and half human; that they were linked to the spirit world because they dig below the earth each autumn and come back out of the earth each spring. A bullshit stupid myth, Trapper thinks.

Fact: a bear just rising from the so-called spirit world doesn't have any gastric juices in his stomach yet. Trapper's killed bears just coming out of hibernation and has opened their stomachs out of curiosity, and found live ants crawling around in the empty stomach, ants that the bear had licked up ten, twenty, maybe thirty minutes before Trapper came sauntering through the woods.

Trapper's building a hide boat: tanning and stretching the wolf hides on the banks of the river and cutting green willow limbs. Maybe the boat will float and maybe it won't. He wonders why the Indians didn't think birds, like loons, belonged to the spirit world, diving under the water, and then flying into the air. Or maybe they did. Maybe the Indians thought everything belonged to the spirit world.

When he finishes the hide boat, he looks at the huge stack of hides he is going to have to leave behind. He could try and cache them, he knows, but something — wolverine, or bear — would find them soon enough. A damn shame. He piles branches and grass around the stack of rich furs, and chips stones until a spark catches. Soon the hides are a billowing black crackling pyre, like a small volcano on the gravel riverbank.

Trapper trembles but without feeling as he watches the black smoke, as he watches the ghosts of the animals return to the sky. There *is* no spirit world, he thinks. There is just her, whom he wants to capture, on the other side of the river. If he can capture her — that blur through the forest, that movement in the corner of his mind's eye — all will be made new again.

Spirit world, my butt, he thinks, turning to look at the river. He loads his traps into the round boat, readies the paddles he's cut and carved, and pushes out into the rapids. The river is wild with the loud underwater clunks of rocks tumbling against one another. It's so frigid that he won't even live long enough to drown if the boat capsizes.

He rows like crazy, his small violet eyes fixed firmly on the far shore. He feels the rocks clacking beneath him, the force of this one river on this one immense earth. Rapids drench him, slicking back his thin white hair. He watches the shore without blinking. Remembers, in a glimpse, Uncle Harm's mangled face.

Remembers a coyote he saw running off with one of his drags. The coyote was too smart to try and pull the drag, a grappling hook, through the brush, where it would get hung up. Instead, the coyote carried the drag-hook in his mouth, running along on three legs, that fourth foot flopping whenever the trap hit the ground, but running, and he escaped: looking back at Trapper with that one foot raised and the drag in his mouth.

Pulling hard on the oars. The far shore closer now, close enough to see small blue flowers blooming on the bank. And the smell of the woods: *her* woods.

5

It's spring, and bears are coming up out of the earth. For twelve days they have staggered through the woods like drunk sailors. They can't quite wake up, and their eyesight — poor to begin with — is worse than ever. They walk into trees and fall over. The bears stretch and yawn, as if trying to wake up, and they're exceedingly dangerous at this time. Trapper moves through the woods with caution, head down, looking for Judith's curved tracks. He allows himself to think of her breasts, which remind him of apples.

Bears are staggering through the woods and roll on their backs, trying to stand up straight, and Trapper says to one,

"Brother, I know how you feel," and passes right by it. Remembers that the Indians revered the grizzly so much that they wouldn't even speak the bear's name, whether out in the woods hunting it or back in camp talking about it.

Instead, they would give the bear goofy names like "Grandfather," "Good Father," "Worthy Old Man," "Illustrious One," and even "The Master."

Master, my ass, Trapper thinks, stepping around another wobbly bear just up from the earth. The bear is spitting up a small pile of sticky wet green leaves, having eaten too much, too fast, in its lust for the new life.

He knows he should kill them and skin them out, but the hide's no good for trading in the spring.

For a week he sees bears rolling drunk in the woods, as they try to get oriented.

"You're lucky, friend," he says to another. "You're going to get better."

Trapper's still twitching. He has it firmly in his mind now that Judith can save him. That she will lay her hand on his forehead and the shakes will go away.

In Arizona, after making love to her, Trapper would get a washcloth and dip it in a basin of cool water. Then he would come over to the bedside and draw it slowly up the length of Judith's panting body, starting at her summer-dusty toes and drawing it slowly up her hot legs, over the mound of her sex, tickling, and like a sheet, across her concave belly, and like a wet curtain across her breasts.

Up to her chin. Over her closed eyes.

Patting her sweaty forehead with the wet washcloth.

It was too long ago. He can never get back to that. But he's got to chase it. That feeling of not being weak. Of being anything but weak.

Even numbness is better than being weak.

Trapper stops and rests often. He finds her tracks here and there: faint depressions in the moss. He suspects that she is staying within this one forest, that it has somehow become her new home (No! he thinks, dammit, *I* am her home!) and that she is reluctant to leave, to be driven off.

He also thinks she wants to be trapped; if only so she can try to escape again.

There's a strange *wormy* feeling in his mind, and he can hear a buzzing, like night katydids. I love my prey, he thinks, forcing himself to his feet.

Bear, lynx, and lobo all have a round, plump pad on each foot, but the older the animal, the flatter the pad wears until the ball is finally all gone and no pad at all is left — just a flat space.

The female lynx has a shorter and smaller second toe on the hind foot than the male, and her front feet are a little rounder and neater than the male's. The female lynx carries her young farther back in the body than any other wild animal. If she is heavy with kittens, the outside toe on both hind feet spreads out.

Trapper studies the ground, and tries to catch Judith's scent. At one spot, near a small hot spring where he feels certain she's been bathing, he finds one of her club tracks in the moss and puts his nose in the depression and sniffs, closes his eyes and sniffs, but she's clever . . . the sulfur odor of the spring confuses all scent, all instinct. Trapper has it in his mind that her beautiful shimmering yellow hair, which he so loved to brush, is a nest for static electricity, for glimmering ions leaving a magic, charged trail of *cleanliness* wherever she's passed. If he concentrates hard enough on it, he thinks, he can follow this trail. And he's tempted to track her that way — with passion, with desire, which he hasn't felt in a long time.

Trapper wants to *lunge* through the woods, hunting her hair-trail with this new, ten-years-gone passion; but remembers how Uncle Harm taught him to hunt, and how he has always hunted — giving himself over to the mindless, the barbaric, and shunning the mistakes of passion, regret, guilt.

"A hunter slipping up on a moose," Uncle Harm had preached, his face gouged and raked like the craters of the moon, but invisible in the darkness of the back porch — his white linen suit all they could see in his rocking chair, and his white Panama hat — "will make the animal uneasy by 'concentrating' his mind upon the animal.

"Those who would catch a woodsman of the old school asleep do well to come carelessly," Uncle Harm said. He'd been halfway like the Indians, in that respect, calling animals things like "woodsmen of the old school." Trapper had heard him refer to one grizzly as "Golden Friend of Fen and Forest" and had had to ask him what the hell he was talking about.

It was when Harm started getting really old, Trapper remembered, that he began to develop all the *respect:* all that Golden Friend shit. Trapper knew it for what it really was: fear. Coyote fear.

Still, there had never been a better trapper than Judith's Uncle Harm.

"A stealthy approach," Harm had preached, "seems to establish some telepathic communication with the subconscious mind of one who lives with nature. This faculty is borrowed from the animals, and is common among Indians."

Harm was a savage, Trapper thinks. He wore a fancy-ass suit in the evenings, but all he was was a *savage.* Wouldn't fool with doctors. If he got a wound and it became infected, he would lie down in the shallows of the creek, would crawl out into the reeds and let the minnows come in and nibble away the afflicted flesh, and clean it that way.

A savage, with a heart too hardened by killing, he thinks.

Flowers. Women like flowers. This time I will keep fresh flowers on the table.

From the ridge above, standing in a grove of budding-out birch trees, Judith watches as her young-old husband moves in a slow circle in the woods around the hot spring, carefully setting leg-hold traps just under the old rotting leaves. She watches him crouch and sniff at her new-bathed tracks; watches his smashed hands touch the tracks, watches him lower his nose to the tracks once more and sniff.

Despite herself, Judith lifts her hand to her hair, and touches it, strokes it once.

At night, she hears him howling in her woods. *Her* woods! She feels the hairs on the back of her neck rising.

*

He's trembly, but he knows he could outrun her, if only he could catch *sight* of her. Her scent is everywhere. He'd chase her toward a ridge and catch her going up it; Trapper's legs are thick, like a bear's, so that he goes faster charging uphill than downhill.

The Eskimos hunt birds with bolas, little balls of ivory or bone at the ends of strong sinew cords at least a yard long. The hunter whirls at least half a dozen over his head and hurls them among a flock of geese or ducks so that the balls will spread out in their flight. One of them is always sure to tangle itself around the wing or limb of a bird and send it crashing to the ground.

Trapper fashions bolas in the afternoons, resting his tired legs, lying in wait by the hot spring.

Judith watches from the ridge, furious. She slips down to the river and must wash her hair in the cold glacier-silt water. It's not the same as her spring.

Trapper can sense Judith's anger, and knows he's being watched. He smiles.

Why won't he leave me alone? Judith wonders. All I want is my life.

*

God, that Uncle Harm was a numb bastard, Trapper thinks as he whittles on the bolas. He remembers a game he and

Harm used to play — a game that Uncle Harm taught him — called sleep-a-night-and-die.

They'd whittle long, slender, barbed shafts of bone and fit them into a socket at the end of juniper arrows. Then they'd sit on the porch and wait for some small animal to come out of the willows — a nose-wrinkling rabbit, a dusk-wary coyote, even a gentle doe.

They'd fire their sleep-a-night-and-die arrows at their intended victim, proud to be killing not with the machinery of guns and traps, but just *killing*.

Shot into a deer or rabbit or coyote, the barbed point would separate from the arrow socket, floating free in the flesh, and go searching for some vital part with each fleeing step of the creature; it would rankle and twist with each step, ever enlarging and irritating the wound, until the animal died.

*

A myth of bears, Trapper thinks: they'll bring others of their own kind, caught in a trap, food, to ease their hunger, to give comfort. Wolves, yes — he'd seen that often — but never bears.

*

If she's not coming to water at the hot springs, Trapper thinks one moonless night — his wormy mind barely moving in his sleep, like the slow coils of a snake on a cold day — then she must be going to the river.

He rises in the night, crosses the ridge, and sets some new traps and snares. Builds a deadfall, too: not too big — he doesn't want to *kill* her, he says to himself, confused — but big enough, by damn, to hold her.

Then goes back to sleep: to dream of animals attacking him.

*

Judith wakes on the riverbank, listening to the spring sounds of the geese heading back north — snow geese, Arctic geese. If Trapper approaches, she thinks, she'll simply leap up and dive into the cold river and swim away. She'll swim for a hundred years, if she has to. She'll get away, or die trying. The water is so cold. She doesn't think she could make it, but she'll try, if she has to.

At dawn she rises and looks at the river and considers building her own raft: leaving her woods. She listens to the river's lovely roar, feels the great and terrible force, feels it in the gravel at her feet. Leans her head into the river, dips her head under, and washes her hair: scrubs the ions away.

All forests should have at least one man and one woman in them, Judith thinks, as she washes her hair. They are on the same side of the river now, but there is still that other river that separates them . . . and it is no good. We spend our silly lives crossing back and forth over that river, she thinks, rather than swimming *in* it, being carried downstream in whatever manner the drifts and great force will take us.

All forests deserve one man and one woman, Judith thinks, but this man is crazy, has gone over to some other world, and this woman, she thinks — *this woman*, standing up and leaning her head back and squeezing the water out of her hair — is going back downstream. Maybe not all the way to Arizona, but somewhere. Someplace.

The new birch leaves are rattling in the breeze. She will climb the ridge and look down on the poor sick shell of her husband, the past of him, one more time.

How many others have fallen to Trapper in this manner, betrayed by curiosity, and a moment's hesitation — a tempering of what was previously brute fear and headlong, terrified flight? He's caught five hundred lynx by fastening a glittering strip of metal above the trap. And though it is not of his planning, it works this way for Judith; while watching Trapper — that one last look — she does not pay enough attention to herself or where she is going, and walks right beneath his deadfall: bumps the branch holding it above her.

Despite herself, she cries out in pain at how it has crushed her; and he hears the thump of the log landing on her, and hears her cry — *What was that?* he wonders. *Lion? Wolf? Lynx? Could it be her?* — and he starts up the ridge toward the sound, eager-hearted, young again.

And caught under the deadfall, with her shoulder broken, her leg in a leather snare, waiting for him to approach, unable to twist and look back at the river below her, but hearing it, hearing it, what Judith is thinking as she imagines his approach with the club, is this: I know he *loves* me.

Maybe he's changed, Judith thinks.

She can't move a muscle. The river roars.

Maybe he's *well,* Judith thinks.

Then she thinks about the myths of bears, versus the facts. She debates: freedom, or hope? Quitting — *flight* — or pushing on? Does her freedom — river freedom — even exist?

She gnaws at the snare. It takes her a long time, but she's able to pull free of it. This notion, coming seemingly from nowhere, that he still loves her, is confounding her efforts.

The log's so heavy. She can't lift it. With her broken shoulder she tunnels away at soft earth and then gravel, scoops out a depression barely deep enough to slither out from under the big log.

The river is just below. She hears Trapper coming up the other ridge, howling. Judith careens through the trees, running for the river, tripping and falling, her arm and shoulder sticking out crookedly like a bird's crippled wing. Her big curved feet keep tripping her, but she's up and running each time she falls, the earth sending jolts of pain up through her jaws and into her ears.

The diamond rushing waters of the river glitter.

There won't be time to build a raft.

She hits the water as she hit the window the night she busted out of the cabin, but this time he is right with her, on top of her, and is hauling her back out of the river.

She thrashes, broken-armed, like a bird: starts to strike at and bite him, but sees, in a glimpse — a passing shadow, a passing wave of light — a thing almost like tenderness, even concern, in his face, and she does not strike or bite. She pauses, held in his grip.

She feels some part of her escape with the current — her other life, the mythical one. She feels, too, the second life — the real life, also just as mythical — the one he has in his grip once more.

"Listen," he says. "I'll be nice. I missed you. Listen," he says, stroking her hair as if he means to scalp it. "Oh, I love you," he says.

They fall back into being as they were before: as if caught in some cycle too powerful and terrible to escape. As if they might as well be trying to escape the seasons.

He sleeps with his hand tight on her wrist. He doesn't get better, but he doesn't die, either. They just settle into the soil, and their lives again, like rotting trees, and the world passes over them. They keep on trapping things.

Judith dreams for a month or two of how things might have been if she'd hit the river a step or two sooner, but then those dreams fade, as if they are far downstream now, or eroded, or forgotten.

I probably would have drowned, she thinks. I probably would not have made it.

She goes back to the old life, helping him tend traps. She feels cut in half, but strangely, there is no pain.

"Say it again," she tells him, nights when she thinks she must hit the window again at full stride: "Say that you love me."

"Oh, I do," he says, stroking her hair. "I do."

"Say it," she says, gripping his wrist.

Where the Sea
Used to Be

"Daily it is forced home on the mind of the geologist, that nothing, not even the wind that blows, is so unstable as the level of the crust of this earth."

— Charles Darwin

THEY MET BEFORE MIDNIGHT AT THE HOUSE OF THE richest man in Mississippi, and left shortly thereafter with a dark leather country doctor's satchel that was bulging with money, bulging as if trying to breathe, swollen like a dying fish's gills: they were unable to even shut it all the way. There was no moon. Because one of the dogs was sick they had to drive slowly, and the old man had to urinate every forty minutes. The truck was old, because they did not want to appear conspicuous. They had coffee in Starkville, urinated in Columbus, and crossed over the state line of Alabama at dawn. The sun was orange and promising as they came down through the tall pines; no traffic was on the road yet, and there was smoke in only a few of the chimneys, rising blue and straight. It was October.

"I like to be traveling at this time of day," Harry told Jack. Harry had slept between stops the entire drive. Soft fog blanketed the lowest meadows; Holsteins and Angus grazed. It had rained in the night, lightly, before their arrival: that smell was in the air. The road was black and narrow and wound down through the heavy trees, and there was greenness in the small meadows that had been cleared by hand, and by mule, the stumps burned. Fieldstones were stacked around the boundaries of the meadows. There were old barns and tool sheds.

"You can rip up those nasty barns and make picture frames of 'em," Harry told Jack, and laughed. "People in the city'll pay money for those things." He eyed the occasional ancient shed with a steady, labored look as they passed each one, pausing in his heavy breathing, not even hawking phlegm, so that Jack was alarmed into picturing them driving out into the field, hooking up to the porch or a window frame with a rope, and driving off, pulling the scatter of buildings down like dominoes. Stacking the wood in the back of the truck. Driving on, deeper into the heart of Alabama, to enter, to take. Harry was seventy-two, the boss. The peace and freshness of the morning made Jack not mind anything. His life was set before him. The dogs awoke and began tumbling about in the back: jawing, yipping, fighting. The poor one feeling better.

The sun rose over a hill as they reached the Vernon city limits. Harry said he was hungry. They were on an expense account. He ate six eggs and three biscuits. Jack fed and watered the dogs and scratched their ears. Dudley had said the dogs would be as valuable as the satchel. People still thought Dudley could find oil. It was the last hurrah.

The dogs had been purchased late the afternoon before, from the Animal Rescue League, and were along because there was a man who was already working up in north Alabama, a man named Wallis Featherston, who had a dog, and the people whose oil and gas leases he was buying knew, or believed, they could trust a man who loved dogs. Wallis had worked in a menial job for Dudley Estes for several years, but was now on his own, taking small bits and pieces of leases and then selling his ideas to other, larger companies, larger than even Old Dudley — companies that Dudley wanted some day to equal: Shell, Phillips, Texaco — who would go in and buy the remaining leases in the prospect and drill the wells, and Wallis would be able to participate for a percent or two or three. It was said that Wallis was getting his leases very cheaply, because he was country, like the people he was leasing from — bone raw and country, rusty and gravel, a people of cold winters, rainy springs, and hard farming — and Wallis had a dog, which rode around with him everywhere. Wallis had a plane, too: he flew around, looking at things.

So Harry's and Jack's boss, Old Dudley, had decided to go with what worked. Old Dudley was sixty years old, a billionaire, and for some reason was chasing this ex-clerk: trying to catch up with his successes in the oil fields. Wallis was twenty-eight, and slept in a field in his sleeping bag, or in the truck, when it rained. He hadn't participated in a dry hole yet. He'd hit on thirteen straight wells. He had named his dog Dudley.

Jack ordered ham for breakfast. The sausages and hams were good up in these hills. The farmers wore overalls and straw hats and spoke with nasal twists and risings of the language, and still used mules, red championship ones from Tennessee. The country was too tough for tractors. There were also sawmills, a few.

Jack smiled at one of the waitresses. None of the girls were pretty, and they all looked the same, like a hundred plain sisters. He would find one, though, an outsider, passing through, like himself. She would be smitten with the promise of youth and the adventure of his working for Old Dudley. There was a heavy padlocked chain around the satchel. The key to the lock was on a necklace over Jack's chest. The key against his skin felt like a woman's hand, sometimes; the heat. It made him dizzy. He wanted to do good, for Dudley. The dogs barked and played, outside. People went to the window and asked what kind they were.

*

Wallis sat out in the field where he camped, with his maps in his lap, checking leases. A landowner in the area, a woman, brought him some lunch: chicken, creamed corn, biscuits, all of it still hot. It was in a straw basket with a cloth over the top. People were discovering the basin: it hadn't been drilled for over seventy years. The day was bright, and there was newness; you could smell oil in the air, too. No one knew where it was coming from — there were no wells in the area, hunters had never found any seeps along the creeks — but it had the heady smell of live oil, black. Dudley had drilled eight dry holes in the little valley. Wallis loved to lunch there often. He had saved the dog Dudley from being killed by a bird hunter: speechless, furious at the dog's ineptitude, his inability to point birds, the man had been aiming his gun at the dog when Wallis, out walking, came up on them. Wallis bought the dog for all the money he had in his pocket, a dollar and sixty-seven cents, and named him Dudley, because he couldn't hunt.

*

"It's a hot summer," Wallis said aloud, to himself. Though it was mid-October, it seemed coldness would never come. In the warmth everything tasted good. He shut his eyes. There had to be some trick; he had to be missing something. He was too happy. There was very much the urge to be cautious: to suspect a fall.

He flew: long, lazy circles over towns and woods, flying low and slow: peeling an apple as he flew, sometimes. Looking for the thing, the thing no one else knew to look for yet, though he knew they would find it, and rip it into shreds. He considered falling in love.

*

He sat on the porch of people's houses, and discussed leisurely the business of finding oil. He scratched his dog's ears, and talked hunting. He ate dinner; he took their leases, writing a personal check, and became friends with the people. His jeans and shirts were always clean. He didn't worry about his happiness too much. It was always there. He could count on it. In the years 1902, 1903, and then again in 1917, there had been some wells drilled in the basin. Then nothing for years and years. Now they were coming back. His heart had been broken, like anyone else's, so very long ago, and unfairly. It didn't matter now. He didn't even think of her name anymore. It didn't even matter, now.

The basin was an ancient, mysterious, buried dry sea: scooped out deep into the old earth more than three hundred million years ago and then filled slowly with sand, from an old ocean, waves lapping at empty shores — an Age of Sharks, thousands of varieties of sharks in the warm waters in those days — hundreds of miles of empty beaches, a few plants, windy days, warmth, no one to see anything, the most mysterious sea that ever was — and then, slowly, the sea had left again, and the dunes, the bays, were covered up by millions and millions of years: swamps first, then deserts, then mountains, then river country, carrying parts of the mountains back down to the same sea, older, farther south . . .

The basin and its history lay hidden, and no one ever knew it was there, and the oil and gas from all its lives and warmth were only two thousand feet below the green and growing things of the present. It had been ten thousand feet below, at one time, but erosion and time were stripping back down, coming back closer to it, as if trying to get back to the old beaches, and those times.

The woods were full of pine trees. The hills were steep: they stretched up into the Appalachians, they were the foothills, crumpled, of the Appalachians. The people were terribly wiry and most of them had never seen a beach. Wallis had helped discover the basin's existence. When he walked through the woods and it was quiet, he tried to imagine the sound the old waves had made: miles and miles of empty beach: nothing there, nor would there be, ever. Doomed, and sealed. A beach missing something, but beautiful. Pine straw beneath his feet.

*

A late night in one of the three little restaurants in Vernon: Harry and Jack, eating again, dessert and coffee, the only ones in the place, save for waitresses: near closing time. Going over some leases to be looked at the next day. The money bag, chained to the table, at their feet.

"Get what you can," said Harry, eyes merry, leaning forward over his stomach: waiting, for Jack to join in, and finish the singsong phrase he'd made up.

"Can what you get," said Jack tiredly.

Harry laughed and leaned back. "Poison the rest!" he cried. Tears came to his eyes. Old Dudley's strategy regarding the newfound basin was less than brilliant, but effective: if they leased everything that was available, then surely some of it would contain oil. Harry thought Wallis's string of successful wells, of having never participated in a dry hole, was a little dainty, foppish.

"These little pissant two- and three-acre leases," he growled. "Shit almighty, a man can't make a living off those things. Shit almighty he can't even buy groceries on them. He can just barely get his money back, so he can go out and buy another two acres." They had tied up, for ten years, over a thousand acres belonging to a family called the Stanfords that afternoon — they would probably never drill it — and another hundred and fifty from the Woodvilles, for five years.

Harry ordered another piece of pie. "A man that won't take a risk on what he believes in, and sink it all on one well — a man like that, who can't take a big lease, has got a short hooter."

He cut into the second piece of pie, breathing hard.

*

Wallis lived in the field, had been in the field for three years, since the time he left Old Dudley's employ, and he liked it: the smells. He rolled his maps out on the hood. Only on the very hardest of freezing nights, or sometimes for a day or two in the middle of a drought-filled summer, would he come into town and get a room at Mrs. Brown's Motel. He didn't have much money. There was some good income from the few wells he was in, but he turned it all back into still more leases. Mrs. Brown let him use her typewriter when he was ready to make a lease final. Neither of them ever had money. Mrs. Brown was sixty-five and her husband had been killed in a mugging one night at the motel desk four sad years ago. The car that got away had Illinois plates and they never saw it again. Mrs. Brown had a gas well on her land that Wallis had helped get drilled. The rooms were $16.50 a night, and she let him keep Dudley in his room.

Mrs. Brown was violently cheerful. She lived in the motel office, had a small kitchen and folding sofa bed back there, a television and a coffee maker, and it was almost as if she were waiting for the muggers to return.

"Evening," Wallis would say, when he came into the office. Bells would jangle over the threshold: a warning signal.

"Right," Mrs. Brown would say. Grief had made her grim, and she smiled like a skeleton. If she tried to speak even an entire sentence it would dissolve and there would be tears. She had loved her husband beyond what was healthy. Wallis was a little wary, uneasy, sometimes, around Mrs. Brown. But he liked her.

"Cold," Wallis would say, grinning at her.

"Single digits," she would say, the lower lip trembling between the two words: the challenging smile, leading with her chin. Daring anyone to say she was not happy. Wallis would become a little too sad to talk to her for very long.

*

Harry and Jack always stayed there. They used up all the hot water when they took their long showers. Anyone staying in the motel could hear Harry's wet coughs, his violent hacks. Wallis would read with Dudley's head in his lap, and sometimes his thoughts would drift, and he'd wonder,

wonder hard, about Jack: picturing himself — briefly, for a few almost unimaginable seconds — the way one sometimes imagines being in jail — holed up in that room with Harry.

The coughs would burst out into the night: almost exactly when the ringing from the last one had just disappeared, thinned away to nothing, and the beautiful night silence and clarity of Alabama blackness was beginning to build back up — smoke, up in the hills above town, from old chimneys; yellow blazes of window light, comfortably and widely scattered over the hills, some hills larger than others — only then would the next cough, like something expelled, blat out. It was on one of these sleepless nights that Wallis realized Harry was dying.

He tried to picture Dudley, the other Dudley, at the funeral, but could not. He knew that Harry had family. Doubtless they pictured him a hero: gone for weeks at a time, on the great hunt, seeking riches. The wind blew hard over the motel. Dudley slept soundly. Wallis lay on his back with his hands behind his head and listened to Harry cough. He had a little more respect for Jack, but he still couldn't understand why Jack would take such a job, would work for and with such a man. The wind blew harder. Limbs and branches began to land on the roof, and finally, the sounds of the coughs were carried away, and lost.

Wallis dreamed about what it was like to be out there when the well was tested, and the proof — the oil itself — terrible, powerful, smelling good and very hot, came rushing up the hole: proving that you had been right.

*

The town was too small. He couldn't avoid them all the time; they ran into each other now and again. Dinner at dusk in the cafeteria with the buffet on Wednesday nights. Tables near each other: Harry speaking across two tables.

"Why'd you leave Dudley, boy?" he asked, pausing with his mouth full. There were field peas and grits and all sorts of things in it. The waitress blanched and left that area of the room. Jack looked down at his plate and clenched his jaws. He wanted girls, oil, money, respect. He'd do anything for it: sell himself to Dudley, live with Harry. He played with his cornbread vaguely, scooted it around on his plate, and leaned slightly forward to hear Wallis better.

"I learned how to find oil," Wallis said. He could have been saying he had learned how to tie his shoelace. It didn't hold any intrigue for him, and that puzzled Jack.

Harry was mesmerized by oil, and thought all geologists were witches, shamans, fakes. He could only believe that which was in him.

Jack looked at Wallis and could feel the thing that was different in Wallis, but didn't know it had a name. There was confusion. Wallis seemed pretty much like a loser to Jack. Wallis would lose, he thought. And yet when he looked at Wallis the chain around Jack's neck felt heavy: as heavy as if the entire satchel was hanging from it.

Harry paid for Jack's meal: he told Wallis he'd have to get his own, being competition and all.

The two men laughed, going out the door. Wallis finished his tea.

*

There was a pretty girl in town. Her name was Sara. She'd lived in the valley all her life: lived it above the oil. She was twenty, and she wanted to go places. Sara looked at the money truck a long time when it rumbled down the roads, raising dust — the odd young man with the necklace driving it, the old man riding at his side, and in the back, the two hounds they never seemed to pay any attention to — but also, she laughed at it, after it had passed her by. They had already drilled on her land. Harry Reeves's old puppeteer, Dudley, had drilled on her parents' land — a German family, the Geohegans were tremendous landholders, owning more than eight thousand acres — and the well had been dry. They drove past her every time now. She went down to see Wallis: everyone knew where he camped. This in the summer. Her hair was soft.

"How many wells have you drilled?" she asked him. He was sitting on the wing of the plane, looking at his notes. Wallis knew who she was, and where she was from, and about her parents' well. He was surprised their well had been a dry hole, and he believed, knew, that the rest of the land beneath their lease held oil. He considered the nuances of revenge. He bit into an apple. She boldly handed him a piece of cheese she had brought, like a student having come for a good grade — she held it out as far as she could, for him to take. He accepted it, sliced it with his knife, looked up at her with the sun behind her. He handed her a piece back. He did not have enough money to lease all of the Geohegan's land. He had found too much oil, this time. He did not know her name, only who she was.

"Thirteen," said Wallis. He decided to keep it quiet, about the oil beneath her. To wait until he could afford to drill the whole thing. To sting Dudley. It would be a big well: the biggest in the county, the most the old sea could give.

"Thirteen?" she said, softly. Her hair was blond, down in a braid. She wore a light blue dress. There were faint freckles on her nose. Thirteen wells did not seem like a lot.

"I've never drilled a dry hole," Wallis said. It was funny, he thought, for him to say that. It made the apple taste bad.

He reached into his truck and pulled out a thermos: shared some warm water with her. She brushed her hair back, as if the wind was in it, and watched him. Lamar County, in the state of Alabama. There were bears in her woods. Her parents raised chickens, and had many cattle. It was unbelievable that he had a plane. She didn't think she'd look at the money truck, not anymore.

He had mapping to do that day. She stood back and watched him take off, bumping down the long field; when he was hazy in the distance, the plane left the ground. She shielded her eyes. He disappeared over the hill.

*

Dudley, in the warm cockpit, lifted his head and looked at Wallis steadily as the plane flew, gaining altitude. He could tell what was coming.

When they were far above the earth, Wallis banked the plane and then rose into a steep climbing stall, pointing the plane straight at the sun, as he did every day, at least once: the propeller's revolutions becoming weaker and softer, more futile, as the engine strained against the pull of the rocks and mountains and rivers below it: the persistent, wavering squall of the stall horn: hard shuddering, and then the plane, five thousand feet up by now, peeled off to the side, unable to go any higher at that steep a pitch. The nose was pulled abruptly down, as if following an anchor tossed from the window, and the plane went into a spinning dive, like a ride at the fair, straight at the ground, which was visible far below in patches through the clouds. Pencils and erasers and dust flew past their ears, the press of force on their bodies. Dudley was strapped in, as always. His long ears hung out at right angles, as if in space.

When the last clouds were cleared, Wallis pushed the yoke in sharply, about half its length, and pressed one rudder pedal in, to stop the spinning. The plane pulled smoothly out of the dive, and flew flat and straight. Things that were stuck to the ceiling rained back down again. They were going to live. Wallis could do other things with an airplane, too. He did it to stay sharp — so that when there was a thunderhead or wind shear or he got trapped between trees and a power line, too near a radio antenna's guy wires, he would be able to get out: would have the ability to get out.

Farmers and others below who saw him, practicing far out over the larger, wooded hills that rolled up, folding, into the Appalachians like waves of forest, said he was witching: that there was a device or machine in the nose of his plane that could smell oil. Whenever he passed over a large stretch of it, it pulled the plane down toward it, into a dive.

To the country people thereabouts, Wallis was a hero, and risking his life for them. On slow evenings when no other customers were around, he ate free at some of the restaurants. They began to feel badly, sometimes, taking the money from Harry Reeves and Jack: bargaining, dickering. Wishing maybe they could lease to Wallis.

People waved at Wallis and Dudley when they saw them driving, and yet he remained a mystery, unlike other things in the country. Their lives were simple and straight and filled with the work and the talk about crops and the grocery store, and ever, pleasurably, hatefully, always with emotion, the weather; but he was outside these things.

"He's got to be that way," an old man said, spitting, when they talked about him at the gas station. "He's looking for the hardest thing to find in the world. Shit, it's buried: it's invisible."

Heads nodding. They looked up at the sky. He was looking for the invisible thing. He could see things they couldn't.

*

Another time, in a restaurant: breakfast, the three of them in the same room. Early, foggy. He looked at Jack when Jack turned slightly away from him, checking out, paying the cashier. There was no way on earth Jack could *like* Harry, or even tolerate him, or the man Dudley either. It was obvious, even to Wallis, who rarely watched people, that Jack was being a fake, a turd, a brown nose, for some later motive. Everyone knew, Wallis thought, that it was better to belong to yourself and have one acre in a drilling well than to belong to another man, even if that man had a hundred, a thousand wells, or the whole county. This had to be common knowledge, a fact of existence, didn't it? How could one breathe and not know this?

Jack was looking back at Wallis. Wallis realized this but could not turn away. His mouth was slightly open, even: staring. He looked and looked at Jack, frowning with his eyes, trying to get a handle on it but unable to, trying to see beyond, like the old ocean he could see from the sky ... but not this. "Damn," Jack said, and turned away, shaking his head, and left the restaurant, behind Harry, who was carrying the satchel. Wallis watched him go; he gave them a minute to be gone before leaving himself: woodsmoke, when he stepped outside, and the smell of bacon. He rolled his collar up. It felt good to be alone, and in the crisp air.

Later that day, flying, coming down through some clouds, he forgot to pull the carburetor heat switch. The plane looked different to him, and the mountains as well. He had to put down in a field, and when he did, the ground felt different, too. His legs were shaky. He called Dudley and they walked a little ways off from the plane and he lay down in the middle of the field in the sun on his back and closed his eyes, and felt wind, sun, the ground below him. He lay with his back to the ground as a wrestler would, pinning it: he thought what a short distance two thousand feet was, and tried to imagine the oil beneath him, straining to get out, but was unable to. The sun confused him, with its warmth, and brightness. He dozed through the rest of the afternoon. His life meant something. He was his own man, belonged to no one: he had never drilled a dry hole, and he had saved a dog from being killed. There was a balance sheet, and as long as one did not go below zero, it seemed a victory: like continuous, enduring victory.

He was terrified of going below that zero: of belonging to someone else. It seemed that everything bad would follow from that. You would catch emphysema. You would have to wear a chain around your neck. You would have sold yourself, and by the very act of doing it once — though he was sure those who did it told themselves otherwise, that it was only for a little while — you would never, ever be able to buy yourself back. Because there wouldn't be anything left to buy. Not even if you went a little fraction of an inch below that zero. The sea would move in: the old times would be buried.

He fed Dudley, scratched his ears, ate apples in the sunlight and in the plane as he flew, and held on for dear life.

*

He and Jack and Harry were somehow yet again in the same restaurant at the same time, even though it was north of town several miles. Bad luck, thought Wallis, the third time in a month, but also he was not much concerned. He had leased twenty-seven acres in section 13 that day, for a tenth of what it usually cost: that was how he'd been able to afford such a large tract of land. The reason he had gotten it so cheaply was that Old Dudley had drilled a well there several years ago, and had thought it dry, and had plugged it. Wallis had never owned twenty-seven acres in a prospect before. He became near-dizzy at the thought of it. And it would be fun, too, to embarrass Old Dudley, to go in and drill a place that Dudley had left, and find oil. The statement would be stark and obvious: Dudley could not find oil on that twenty-seven acres; Wallis could; therefore Wallis was a better geologist.

He didn't need to be nice to Dudley. He would try hard to stay away from the very natural feeling of revenge because he knew it was a trap, like going below the zero — he had found so much oil for Old Dudley, when he worked for him, unrewarded — and it would cut Wallis up, and beat him, even if it did sound fun and good — questing for vengeance — but neither did Wallis have to be nice to him. If revenge happened, it happened. It was good. He could belch in Old Dudley's company if he wished and not excuse himself. He had escaped Old Dudley, and his life mattered.

The salt and pepper shakers on the tables seemed to have significance and clarity. He watched Jack and Harry muddle along through the buffet: pausing, asking questions of the chef, frowning, rubbing their chins: reaching slowly and hesitantly for this dish and that: pie, beans, chicken — leaning over and reaching as if controlled by strings from above. The air tasted like spring water to Wallis. He got a bowl of oatmeal, a piece of cold melon, and a Coke. He sat at the far end of the restaurant, his back to them — and their backs to his — and ate. The melon was fresh; the oatmeal was hot.

He left a tip and walked out the door. It was good to be able to just take four steps and be out the door: not having to turn around, look back, or pass by them. He drove out to the field with the windows down and took his sleeping bag out and unrolled it on the ground and got in it.

The stars were like Christmas. The night was cold. The twenty-seven acres on his lease application in the glove box made his toes want to dance around in the bottom of the sleeping bag. He supposed that he was getting close to revenge and that was different from flying around eating apples and looking for oil, but also there was the wild and primal goodness of the feeling, visceral, of having scored a killing punch. Something about it made him want to do it again, and maybe again and again. He lay awake for a very long time, pleased with himself, and was enormously happy. The stars seemed to encourage him. As if they were on his side.

*

It got much colder. New Year's Eve saw zero; the next day, twelve below, and windy. Sara and Wallis lay in their bed by the window at the Brown Motel with the lights off and the curtains open. Dudley slept at the foot of the bed: the three of them conspiring to make a beautiful steady breathing. There were stars, more than ever. Wallis held her tightly. They watched the stars for a while, and then she rolled over on top of him and made love to him. She looked at his face the whole time. Blankets covered them; the room was cold. The bed rocked, steadily; Dudley stirred, in his sleep, once. She was imagining that she was atop one of the pumping jacks that went down with the rods and then came back up with a rushing swab of oil. In cold weather the oil sometimes steamed.

He tried very hard to love her. He felt that it was time for him to be in love. That he needed to be in love.

After, he closed his eyes and pulled her to him, and she put her head up under his chin. He would find love. And they, he and Sara, would find the Big Well. Somehow he would get the money together to drill it himself — not paying for 1 percent, or 3 percent, but the whole 100 percent, start to middle to finish — he did like *that* idea — and then he would try. There would be a house in the woods, with Dudley the hound that couldn't hunt, and they'd have a child, and Wallis would work very hard at loving her the way he thought it *should* be, the pure way, the way he found oil. If only he could love her the way he looked for oil: it would be perfect. He'd try.

Around midnight, a fierce, jagged coughing began. The sounds traveled through the cinder blocks from about three rooms down. Wallis listened to the sound of Old Dudley running a young man and an old one down to their deaths. Sara awoke, not knowing where she was, reaching for a lamp.

"What's that?"

"Harry and Jack," he said.

"Is there oil on my land?" she said, suddenly. She had his shoulders in her hands: she was over him again. He looked away, at the dark wall, and listened to Harry's coughs. It sounded as if he were standing upright now, waddle-pacing the room; an old death stagger, Wallis imagined — Jack probably with his head under both pillows. It was very possible that Wallis couldn't love anyone: could only work, and work. He knew there were people like that.

"Maybe," he said, getting up angrily, leaving her grasp and pulling on a pair of underwear: Dudley rising, startled, at his heels, not knowing this routine, but with him. Wallis and Dudley went quickly out the door, and barefooted, shivering violently already from the weather's strength, Wallis hurried across the gravel, reached Harry's door, and began kicking it. There wasn't any moon. The wind carried the thumps of his kicks quickly off. A light came on: Jack's face through the crack of the door, the chain beneath his chin like the chin strap on a football helmet.

Wallis put his face in the wedge of light so that he was an inch away from Jack's startled eyes.

"Shut that shit up or kill the old man," he said. Dudley growled and raised his hackles: he stood as big as a wolf.

"I . . . I . . . I'm sorry," Jack said.

"It keeps Mrs. Brown awake," Wallis said. He didn't say anything else, just stood there. Jack could see the squareness and hardness of his teeth, and the thing that was in the bottom of him, in the bottom, far bottom, of everyone.

"We'll . . . he'll stop," Jack said.

"I'm going to cut his throat out, tonight, if he doesn't," Wallis hissed. "I'll either come through the door or the window. There'll be blood all over the sheets."

He walked hurriedly back to his room, and barely made it before he could walk no farther. Sara cried out loudly when he got in bed; it was as if a block of ice had been slid in with her.

"Yes there's oil under your land," he said. He was shuddering as if seized by a current.

She came back to him: moved back in closer, held his coolness, tentatively, then all the way: pulled him to her yet again.

"Oh, baby," she said, with her eyes shut.

"Oh, baby," he repeated: trying it out.

He was numb. He warmed slowly.

When he awoke in the morning, he felt thicker, heavier, and later in the day realized it was because he was now carrying two things, anger and revenge. Logic, and having worked for Dudley — having seen everything done the *wrong* way — told him that the angrier he got at not being able to fall in love with Sara, the less likely it was that it would happen — but he had exploded at Jack and Harry, and now, walking, he felt as if it — anger, and pride — was building up again. He felt as if he were oil, far below the ground, trapped in a thin layer of rock. He felt that when the drilling bit did hit his formation, and pierced the very top of it, he would come out: blowing, all of it, a fire, a roar. That he would burn down whatever it was that had touched him, and diluted him. Dizzy, he bent down and scratched Dudley's ears. The day was clear and cold: the light was pretty. He knew that you could only do one thing well: to do it the right and best way. There could be nothing else. His boss was too good at making money, whether off of other people's woes or not, to be a good geologist. Wallis was too good at what he did, feeling what used to be, to make money. He knew about the old ocean. He could see it, and felt he had lived on it. He had its number.

He wondered if he could even drill a dry hole: if he could stop wanting to find oil.

He wondered if she was worth it.

*

She came driving up just as he was climbing in the plane that afternoon — jeans, tennis shoes, a heavy old blue sweater, and a parka: her hair, in the sun. She hugged him, standing under the high wing of the plane to do so. Her

face felt cool and smooth, like he imagined love was supposed to. She smelled good, and he wanted her.

Surely, thought Wallis, if love was not capable for him
with this girl, then it could not exist, for him.

He took her up. He was jittery: flushed, as when he first
realized he was tracking oil. (When he actually found it,
pinpointed it, mapped, and contained it, he was cool — it
was anticlimactic, by that point — but the first scent — the
turn of the head, the question — that was the rush.)

She took her parka off. She took her shirt off. The sun
was warm in the cockpit.

"Show me you're a very good pilot," she said, laughing.
It happened to everyone: it could happen to anyone. It was
the most common thing in the world. She had come out to
see him.

A mile above the earth they made slow, graceful love: he
let her hold the yoke and work the pedals some as they
flew. It alarmed him, a little, to not be able to see in front of
him. It did feel good. He closed his eyes for as long as he
dared. When she began to cry out he took the yoke and began to climb slowly into the sun.

*

She wanted to fly over her parents' farm. She wanted to
drop her bra into the woods, to see if she could find it. She
didn't wear underwear.

"What will happen if it hits someone?" she asked.

"It'll kill them," he said, truthfully. She was poised at
the window, ready to open it, holding the bra in one hand
like a thing soiled. She looked at him, surprised, and then
laughed: the thought of it. And now the excitement: the
risk. Quickly she shoved the window open — the fast suck
of wind — and tossed the bra out. He watched her watch it
go. Her back was still bare and had goose pimples. Her
waist was narrow, with faint gold hairs at the base of her
back. Totally engrossed, she watched the bra get smaller

and smaller. He banked into a tight holding turn, like water spiraling around in a drain, so that she could keep watching. He had found love, his first time out, since the last time. It was no different from anything else in the world, he decided.

Harry and Jack, with binoculars, on a hill deep in the woods, the highest point in the county, watched them circle.

"He just threw something out," Jack said.

"It's a marker," Harry said. He began to cough: bending over. He straightened up. "I've seen 'em do it a million times." He turned to Jack in earnest: believing himself, almost, as he went along. "It's for when the woods are too thick or dense to survey. He's marking where the oil is. They do it in Texas all the time."

Jack watched them circle, and nodded. They would try to find the marker.

*

The Fellowship Church of Vernon gave Wallis a lease for seventeen acres. Wallis wrote to a serviceman in Germany about another sixty-eight acres: a quiet, simple letter, explaining what he was about, what he wanted to do — to go in and drill where Dudley had missed. He got the lease for free. He began to go back and search all of Old Dudley's plugged wells. About half of them seemed, to him, to be good. He took Sara with him often. They climbed to two miles in the plane. She wanted to laugh and cry both: there was so much to be seen. They climbed to three miles, until the engine faltered and their heads felt light and it was hard to breathe — Dudley on the floor, head under his paws, confused — and looked briefly, when there were no clouds, at the big roll of Appalachians: it was easy to see where the sea had ended. The area below them was, quite obviously, the old beach. Beaches. A hundred miles of it, curving and snaking all around, like a serpent, like a thing still, even that day, alive: it seemed to move as they watched it.

Haze, and the sweep of earth curving away over the edge, its lovely roundness: they had left the earth. Three minutes, four minutes, for as long as they dared — five — the sky a rich heavy purple, a color never seen except at that altitude — and then the slow ride down, both of them suddenly aware of the frailty of the little plane; the lightness, and thinness, of the wings, light canvas wrapped around a hollow aluminum frame. The thinness of the thing that kept them aloft.

*

"When he crashes, we go in and top his leases," said Harry. The plane had disappeared from view, even to the plastic drug-store binoculars. "We pay the landowners, beforehand, to lease to us, exclusively, the first day his leases run out."

Jack nodded. It was what he was being taught. The leases were for three years. Harry and Jack tied up the land with five-year leases, but for some reason Wallis never asked for more than three years. Jack counted: both he and Wallis would be thirty-four in three years. He looked at Harry's face, the open mouth — a wetness of saliva rimming his lips, perpetually hungry — as Harry looked heavenward through the binoculars, and was jealous that Wallis owned his own leases. The richest man in the state of Mississippi, the king of the poorest state in the union, was using them to chase a poor young pilot in love across the county, to learn what he was doing. It made Wallis seem like the holder of some kind of magic. It made Old Dudley's terrible money and power seem less.

*

Wallis started to work late into the nights at the courthouse. He got a key from the probate judge so that he could lock up when he was through: midnight, 1 A.M. A peanut butter sandwich for supper, around 7:00, the great ledgers open like biblical testaments, showing years and years of dizzying history; mortgages, leases, foreclosures, dry holes, and producers. He chewed his sandwich slowly, and read them, looked in all the right books. Dudley sat up on top of the counter and watched him, and waited patiently. Wallis was looking for all the leases on old wells that Old Dudley had plugged without testing. He was going to stop looking for oil, purely, and restrict himself to looking only for oil beneath places where Old Dudley had missed it. It would be like slapping his face with gloves: satisfying.

It had been a new feeling for him the other day, an unexpected one, taking the twenty-seven-acre lease that Old Dudley had dropped several years ago. It was a surprise, and wonderful and new, much as flying and loving had been for Sara. He wanted to do it some more. In fact, it was all he wanted to do.

Sara came up to the courthouse with him once, sat on the counter with Dudley and drank a beer, swinging her legs, and watched, but it was far too slow for her.

When he could no longer keep his eyes open, he would call to his dog Dudley, who would leap down from the counter, and he would shut off the lights and lock up and drive back out to the pasture. Sometimes he would build a little fire and fix some coffee and go over what he had found. It was a lonely life. Dudley would sit and watch him and wait for whatever was going to happen next. Some nights there was the sound of coyotes: geese; owls, too. The air was fresh.

*

They flew more and more: everywhere. They did it five hundred feet above the ground: they went lower. They skimmed along over the tops of trees: scattering birds, doves in roost. Sara got to be a fair pilot.

"Can you find oil down on the coast?" she asked him.

Wallis grinned, shook his head. "Nope," he said. "Just up here." His greatness was limited. He thought later how it was odd that he had never asked himself that question. There had never been a desire to look anywhere else. Why would a man want to go into a country he was not familiar with, knew nothing about?

*

He showed her stalls: spins: figure eights. She was delighted, one day, when he rolled. He started leaving Dudley in the truck. More aerobatics, less mapping. Dudley drilled a well on one of Wallis's prospects, one that Wallis had been able to edge into by buying two acres at the edge of it. They went out to visit the well: Sara, her hair long and clean, static against her sweater, flushed, elsewhere in her mind: having just flown.

Old Dudley was out at the well, which was very unusual: Wallis had never seen him on a location, as long as he'd known him. There was word that he hadn't been out to one in ten years. Harry and Jack knew nothing about geology, and were off eating or leasing. Wallis noticed Old Dudley watching him, at times, rather than the progress of the well itself. It was just a little pissant well, one whose outcome could mean nothing, one way or the other, to Old Dudley. He had his chauffeur and stretch limousine, both of which had been flown over from England. Red mud from the thick hills shrouded the limousine's brilliant blackness.

Wallis noticed Dudley still watching him, smiled, gave a little wave, then smiled wider. He was free.

Dudley smiled, gave his little embarrassed half-nod — a tip of the head, almost like a bird beginning to feed — when he recognized Wallis, in jeans and boots — Dudley had on a black business suit and an overcoat. Wallis felt good that Old Dudley was acknowledging, and curious about, Wallis's freedom. He could read Old Dudley, had learned him like a fascinating book: had studied the locations where he had drilled and knew why he did things — and he was confused, then, when Old Dudley turned his look to Sara and almost smiled, as if relieved at something. As if Old Dudley knew some sly and childish secret which he would not tell Wallis but would keep to himself, and be made happy by it. He turned and began walking, with his chauffeur, over to the well: roughnecks up on the derrick floor, looking down, shirtless, muddy, ragged: a few of them wrestling with the drill pipe. A clear blue sky, a warming day.

Wallis's dog bolted: a blur at the edge of the cleared location was a rabbit.

"Yo! Dudley! Get back here!" Wallis shouted. Old Dudley's shoulders stooped, and he half-turned: an expression of genuine surprise, and then disappointment, to see that Wallis was running after a dog. He turned back around and continued walking. The well turned out to be oil: not a pissant well at all, but the largest discovery ever found in the basin.

*

Old Dudley had the chauffeur stop by Wallis and Sara's truck on the way out: the dog, muddy, bounding happily around in the back of the truck, barking at Old Dudley and at the strange long car. Old Dudley rolled his window down so that he could speak to Wallis.

"Maybe we should plug this well?" Dudley looked different: more intense, more predatory — a way that Wallis had never seen him. Wallis leaned slightly closer, curious: never afraid, though the sense of power around Dudley was thick and heavy, malignant, like a bad odor.

"I beg your pardon?" The well had metered out at twelve hundred barrels per day.

Old Dudley chuckled. "I mean, that's a lot of oil: we don't want to glut the market. Perhaps we should wait until prices are more worth our while." Dudley's father had been a farmer, and poor all his life: poorer than Wallis. This time Old Dudley didn't chuckle, and looked straight at Wallis, but Wallis was free. Wallis shrugged, held up his hands. It truly did not matter.

"Why not?" Wallis said. "It's your well."

Old Dudley's face was leaning a little too far out: the anger, if it had been that, had to come back in. He looked tricked, betrayed.

"I mean, for twenty or thirty years," he said. But he was not good at threats, at cruelty. He was only good at making money.

Wallis smiled, shrugged.

Old Dudley watched him for a minute, unable to believe it was sincere, but then he did: the girl, the dog, the old truck. He smiled at Wallis, no longer angry, but thoughtful, nodded to Sara — the tip of an imaginary hat, it seemed — and even glanced at the dog, as he was being driven off, after the window had rolled back up. The well began selling oil that afternoon.

*

On the drive home, Old Dudley thought about purity, and even intensity: how it once had been for him, when he was young and when it truly didn't matter whether a well was shut in, rather than hooked on line, after being discovered: how finding it, rather than selling the oil, had been the only important thing. He was a businessman now, but had been a scientist, in school, and had been impressed with the knowledge that purity could never last, that nothing could ever last: that everything was changing, always. He had made his choice early and had not bothered to waste the energy — for it would have been wasted — trying to preserve the purity. He was sixty and had fifteen or twenty years of life left, and what he was interested in now, after so many years, what he was wishing, was that he had retained a bit of it after all, and its intensity, because he had all the success he needed.

Though he had seen Wallis's leasing activity, on the scouting reports, and was alarmed, slightly, at what it looked like he was doing. As if even his success — not physically, but emotionally — might be spirited from him.

He thought that Wallis would fall back: that he would lose his purity, too.

Dudley had hundreds of employees to think about and hundreds of business concerns, most of them larger and many of them more critical and pressing than what had over the years gotten to be a sideline, his oil activity, particularly in the Black Warrior Basin; but on the drive home, it was Wallis, and purity, and Wallis's truck, dog, and girl that he thought about: thumb and forefinger holding his chin: tenement houses, ragged, scraggly winter cotton remains, and drooping telephone lines whizzing past. Tinted windows: conditioned air. An old black woman in an apron, coming out onto her porch and staring as his limousine passed. The chauffeur, so far up in front of him that an intercom was necessary to communicate. He looked away from the chauffeur, back out the window again, at the delta, and thought about Wallis. He knew that he couldn't have picked a better girl to do it, but also Wallis was no fool, was finding oil, was on to something, and still had the dog and truck.

*

Harry Reeves died on a Sunday afternoon, while driving the money truck: a grim picture it made, him collapsed over the wheel, his heart finally too squeezed by the excess of his flesh. The truck continued to thunder down the mountain along Little Hell's Creek Road making for town — Jack grabbed the wheel, trying simultaneously to pull Harry's deadness away from it — and when Jack put his foot in the vicinity of the brake, jabbing empty space, he got tangled up with Harry's dead legs, and the polyester double-knit. The truck glanced the curb and rolled, spilling dogs, Harry, the spare tire, lug wrench, and the money satchel outside of town: Jack held on to the steering wheel and stayed in the truck.

No one else was around. He got out, amongst the broken glass and hissing. One dog was dead, curled up in the wrong shape, and Harry was stretched out like a dead actor. The other dog was injured and was trying to reach around and lick its hind leg, or bite it — and like the last person on earth, with a raw and stinging patch on his forehead, Jack began walking in circles about the truck gathering up all of Dudley's money: some of it caught in tufts of grass, tumbling across the road, some blown up against Harry, like seaweed against a whale's carcass . . . Two thousand feet above the darkness of what was underground, a sealed, Paleozoic ocean, a silent beach, two hundred and fifty million years of silence, oil, and above it all he walked, picking up money. He wondered if he would get fired. It hadn't been his fault: it had been Harry who had wrecked the truck. He wondered what he would do for a living if he lost his job. The richest man in Mississippi: he was working for the richest man in Mississippi.

*

Wallis was having fried chicken at the Geohegans' when he heard the news. The operator had called to tell Mrs. Geohegan: the mountain phone had a shrill clang that shook the thin walls of the house. He looked out the window to the large pasture and motionless cattle, the wooded creek, and out farther into blue haze and treetops. The chicken was good. The gravy was rich, and had pepper in it. He and Sara and Dudley had played tag out in the yard before lunch. He paused, digesting what he was hearing of the conversation between Mrs. Geohegan and the operator, tasting the food, and was relieved to feel sorrow, and a stillness, like being in the woods alone in the late afternoon. He had been worried by his quest for vengeance, and was hoping — knowing that Harry would die — that when he did, the news would not please him.

It was colder than usual for March under the stars that night. Looking up from his place on his sleeping bag, and with his hands behind his head, he dreamed he was on the beach, the old beach, the one he knew better than anyone else and was born 250 million years too late to see, to know, to walk on — to skip across, barefooted, splashing in the shallows. Warm tidal channels, back dunes, sea oats . . . He thought about what he would do if he did not look for oil. He tried faithfully to think of Sara's kisses: of her eyes looking up at him when he talked about oil . . . the shine in them was similar to the shine of her hair. It bothered him that he could not fall in love with her. Perhaps if he could find one more oil well, a big one, the biggest ever . . . there had to be release in it, eventually.

He was trapped into succeeding, he thought. Maybe if he drilled a dry hole he could be normal.

*

He went to the funeral. Jack's dog was bandaged, looking silly, sitting in the cab of a new blue truck: watching the funeral with a bandage around its waist and head. Wallis went over to the rolled-down window and stuck his head in, let the dog lick it. Jack came over and asked if Wallis could do him a favor: if he could take care of the dog . . .

"Yes," said Wallis, without looking up. He watched the dog lick his hand. The dog was desperate to be loved. The dog was desperate to love. He thought about Old Dudley coming out to test that well. He thought about a prospect in the east portion of the county. The sun and windiness of spring was making him feel light and drawn away from where he was standing. It seemed that every day he could see the old beach more and more clearly: where the dunes were, which would hold oil and which wouldn't, long after they had been buried and forgotten: what the waves had looked like, what the view down the beach had been — the long, straight stretches, and too, the bends, and deep parts offshore . . . He was the only inhabitant in that world, and it was a beach before men, and he liked it: he felt . . . loved. As if the beach had chosen him, for its loneliness. How could he drill a dry hole, when he knew the old empty beach so well?

He flew. The trees and creeks, cemeteries and hills that cloaked those ancient buried beaches didn't bother him. He was seeing his old land. He now only made weak, stabbing attempts at loving Sara. She flew with him: they loved, and afterward, he was looking out the window again; sometimes, and without guilt, he would look out even as it was going on, the love. She wanted to go to Atlanta one weekend, having never been, and he took her. It didn't matter. He found three more wells: small, small interests, but they belonged to him.

She wanted to go to New Orleans, and they stayed in a room high up over the city, a room that smelled of rich times and with mirrors on the ceiling above the bed. He felt detached, far from his shore. At night they walked down to the river, where it went into the sea. A cool breeze lifted off it and came at them. This was his old ocean, cowardly, on the retreat now: some three hundred miles south of where it had once been, in its greatness, inland, when it was brave: the ocean's great advance northward into a place and country it had never been before, and might never return to. He looked out at the river, going into the Gulf, and tried to feel close to it, knowing it was the same . . . but it wasn't. It didn't have that bravery his had had, so long ago. She looked at him questioningly, and took his arm, and they went to eat. She was starting to fall in love with him.

*

She moved in with him: they bought a cabin, on land up above the field where he used to sleep. The austere and churchgoing hillspeople bent the rules for them: Wallis was becoming a champion, and some things seemed right. When he went out to get into his plane, there were often people standing around it, a lot of children, watching, waiting: wanting to know where he was going, that day. What part of the country he was going to check.

When he took leases and did courthouse work — the news had spread that he could find oil in places where Old Dudley had missed it — there were businessmen, undertakers, and monstrous insurance salesmen, seeds of bad earth, leeches who followed him: like puppies, like gulls over a field being furrowed, they tracked him, anticipated, and battled savagely and wretchedly for the small pieces that, like Wallis, they could afford: two acres, fifteen acres, one acre. They used him, and then sat back smiling, and waited, hopefully, for a well to be drilled on their lease. Not understanding, not knowing where the oil was: but knowing that he knew.

He made four more wells the next month: twenty in a row. No one had ever made more than four in a row.

*

Sara still wanted Wallis to drill on her land.

"I can't afford to take your parents' lease," he said, "and with that much land, it's unfair to consider a free lease, even if they would give it. I can't drill it, not yet, not now." He was getting better at the lovemaking: he seemed to be growing into it. He brought her things when she was in the bathtub: a cool wet washcloth to press to her forehead; a mint; a stick of gum. He was surprised to find that he liked to watch her chew gum.

"But there is oil under my land, right?" she asked. Pausing, washing under an arm.

"Right," he said. "A lot of it."

He wanted to touch her face, but drew back. The bathroom seemed empty: hollow. A thing was missing.

*

The twenty-first well, gas, from the very borehole of a well from which Dudley had walked away, three years ago: much gas. A ring for her finger — not wedding, just friendship — but it felt good, when he held that hand. Woodpeckers hammering in the woods above their house. The scold of a blue jay. His picture was in a newspaper, then two magazines. He kissed her in the day, without once wanting to undress her.

*

Old Dudley heard they were living together and was pleased. A little.

*

Once, on a farm far back in the hills, farther than he had ever been before — a glint of sun, on a lake, late in the afternoon, had pulled him there: the plane peeling away, flying him there in short minutes — so far back up into the hills that perhaps it was not even his sea he was feeling — and he touched down, and got out, and walked around for the whole day, feeling something and seeing things but not knowing what was going on. And Jack, in the new money truck, saw him go down, and drove out in that direction, drove all morning, and found where his plane had landed — a gravel road, wide — and Jack went all up and down the side roads, with the satchel, leasing for pennies from people who had never even seen a drilling rig. And Wallis was unable to get even a few small leases before Jack and Old Dudley got all of them. A well was drilled, and it was dry.

Wallis did not leave his territory anymore. He stayed on the ground he knew. And Jack decried him, told all, proud of nothing.

"He was going to lease it, but I stepped in and took the leases before he could, and it was dry. He was going to drill a dry hole."

*

Old Dudley drove up one summer day in the limousine. The sun had suddenly come out about an hour earlier, as if turned on by a switch. Sara fixed him coffee. Old Dudley had a proposition: he wanted Wallis to come back to work for him. Wallis had to think about it overnight before saying no.

Sara didn't say anything. She didn't know what was right, what was wrong. She wasn't sure if she even wanted the well drilled anymore. Old Dudley could have done it in an instant.

Sara's mother came out one day and brought them chicken. Dudley the hound had dug a place out on the side of the cabin where he would curl up and lie down. Sara petted his back, scratched his ears. He played with the other dog, who was healed. The light on their coats and in their eyes was startling, up on the hill, back in the trees, coming down through the leaves. When he drove home in the truck, in the evenings, if he was going back to the courthouse, he would have supper first. Sara would listen for his plane in the afternoons. It did not make sense, but she could hear it even before the dogs could.

*

Two more of Old Dudley's old failures turned into successes for Wallis: one a small well, the other a rushing oil well. He took more leases with the money. He bought Sara a dress that looked beautiful on her.

*

Old Dudley bought Jack a plane. It amused the townspeople. They started giving their leases to Wallis for free: if he would only drill on them. Old Dudley turned sixty-two. He hired a man who was fifty-five to work for him: a geologist, to do the same thing that Wallis was doing, only on larger, fancier maps: scribing his interpretations of the world below onto linen maps with fine calligraphic pens. In the fall, Wallis drilled another well. It was the thirty-fourth well that he had been involved in, but this one, finally, was all his. There was so much gas when he drilled into it that it blew the drill pipe out of the hole, caught on fire, and burned the rig down: a man was killed. Everyone came from miles around to watch the rig burn down. The glow had been visible in eight counties. The earth had trembled and shuddered as the gas blew. Old Dudley came in and leased around him and began making smaller, weaker wells. Wallis didn't have any money again.

Sara kissed him, the night it happened, held him with the lights off, and thought about her parents' farm. She hadn't ever had money before. No one in the county had. She didn't know if money mattered or not.

Jack flew, clumsily, nervously, and dropped flaggings out the window, randomly, trying to make it appear he knew what he was doing, remembering Harry Reeves's wisdom. Shakily, he told Old Dudley that he thought he had it figured, that he thought he knew where they should drill. He'd seen a creek, water bubbling out of a spring: it had to be a fault. They had a rig on it the next week: it made a good little oil well. Jack bought a suit and a gold pocketwatch and watch chain. Even though Old Dudley didn't wear one.

When it rained, Wallis worked in the courthouse, or drove: looked at the trees, and the way they grew. But it wasn't as clear. He couldn't see it all at once. There was no money for a while, only leases, and he paid debts with the dollars coming in from his fractions in his good wells.

"I don't mind being poor," Sara said one evening, mending a shirt. "But I don't want to have any chickens around the house. Every family in this county has chickens, damn it, leaving feathers and bad smells underfoot, and I don't like the sound they make, either." She stamped her foot. There had been no talk of chickens ever before — Wallis didn't want any chickens, either — and he was surprised. It had been five weeks since the rig burned.

"If ever there was a sound of being poor, it's the cackle of chickens," she said. Her parents had always had chickens around the house, even after they were not poor anymore. She was very near tears. He got up and put his hand on her forehead, and stroked her hair.

"No chickens," he said, cheerfully. "All right! No chickens!"

She had to laugh, to keep from crying. He made her laugh often. She had thought she wanted to go places.

She didn't ask him about her parents' land anymore. She thought, sometimes, about the mirrors in New Orleans — everything reversed from the way it really felt.

*

They played games.

"I want to learn how to swim," she said.

He smiled. "When I drill again, next time, and hit, we'll build a swimming pool inside the cabin. We'll heat it. It'll be right next to the kitchen, and we'll add on a room for it."

"I can come straight in from grocery shopping in the winter, set the groceries down on the table, slip out of my clothes, walk down some steps, and dive into the water," she said.

"Nekkid," said Wallis.

"There'll be steam coming up off the water," she said.

They smiled. She tried to picture him working for Old Dudley, as he had, for six years, but could not. They laughed, and joked about Jack flying the little plane. He was clumsy. He bounced the plane like a basketball, on landings. He got lost, often, and all the various towns in the area had at one time or another seen him flying a circle around their water tower, sometimes several times in the same day, trying to find out where he was.

Old Dudley was trying to go back and re-lease all his old acreage, just as a blanket policy: to halt the embarrassment. But there was too much of it, and many people wouldn't lease, to him or to anyone, until they had talked with Wallis: to see if he wanted the lease first, even for a lower price. They didn't want Dudley to drill any more dry holes on their land. The money truck had lost almost all of its charm except to the absolute and very poorest, most desperate few.

Jack wrote a lot of checks for Dudley's leases. There was no longer a need to wear the key on a chain around his neck. But he kept it there anyway, out of habit, and for power.

Springs were beautiful. It rained, and shimmered hot, too, in the summers. Eventually, as Wallis paid more attention to Sara, he drilled a few dry holes. Old Dudley grew aged and feeble, lost his teeth and went into a nursing home: his lawyers declared him incapable and took his business away, gave it to his children. And one day Jack crashed while he was out looking: still dropping white handkerchiefs out the window of the plane, still pretending to see. Wallis and Sara got married in the field. Mrs. Brown died, and the motel closed up, became vacant: weeds, vines. Wallis drilled; Wallis leased. He held on for dear life, to two things, not one — himself and another human being — and did not let go, and never went under zero, not for a day, not for an hour.

Sometimes they would fly down to the coast, near Mobile, land the plane on a lonely stretch of beach, and get out and walk along the shore, in winter: no one else out. He would lean slightly forward, listening to the slow, steady lapping of waves dying into the shore. He would hold Sara's hand. If she tried to speak while he was listening, imagining, he would raise a finger to his lips. The only reason he could have two passions rather than one was because he had never ruined the first. It hadn't ever been sold, when asked for. She watched him watch the beach, the ocean, and considered his success.

The Sky, the Stars,
the Wilderness

"Of all these passers-through, the species that means most to me, even more than geese and cranes, is the upland plover, the drab plump grassland bird that used to remind my gentle hunting uncle of the way things once had been, as it still reminds me. It flies from the far northern prairies to the pampas of Argentina and then back again in spring, a miracle of navigation and a tremendous journey for six or eight ounces of flesh and feathers and entrails and hollow bones, fueled with bug meat. I see them sometimes in our pastures, standing still or dashing after prey in the grass, but mainly I know their presence through the mournful yet eager quavering whistles they cast down from the night sky in passing, and it always makes me think what the whistling must have been like when the American plains were virgin and their plover came through in millions.

To grow up among tradition-minded people leads one often into backward yearnings and regrets, unprofitable feelings of which I was granted my share in youth — not having been born in time to get killed fighting Yankees, for one, or not having ridden up the cattle trails. But the only such regret that has strongly endured is not to have known the land when it was whole and sprawling and rich and fresh, and the plover that whet one's edge every spring and every fall. In recent decades it has become customary — and right, I guess, and easy enough with hindsight — to damn the ancestral frame of mind that ravaged the world so fully and so soon. What I myself seem to damn mainly, though, is just not having seen it. Without any virtuous hindsight, I would likely have helped in the ravaging as did even most of those who loved it best. But God, to have viewed it entire, the soul and guts of what we had and gone forever now, except in books and such poignant remnants as small swift birds that journey to and from the distant Argentine and call at night in the sky."

— John Graves, *Self-Portrait with Birds*

AT FIRST WE EXPLORED THE COUNTRY WITH CRUDE maps drawn by Grandfather on the back of paper bags, but as we got older we used blank maps that we were supposed to fill in ourselves as we went into new places, the deep wild places that Grandfather knew about. He said it was better if we went to those places without maps.

By the time I was ten I knew the names of almost everything I saw, and much of what I could not see. Grandfather said that I was the best granddaughter anyone could ever hope for, but that he would have loved me even if I hadn't loved the woods, and loved the birds. I was five years older than my brother Omar, whom I began to take into the woods when I was eleven. At the time, Grandfather said that I was being raised in the way my mother would have wanted, and I believed that then and still do. My mother chose to live here even after she found out she was sick. She's buried on the bluff four hundred feet above the Nueces River. Father got the map out as she was dying and with Mother's help drew an east-west line and then a north-south line, and in the center of our ten thousand acres was where they decided to plant her. That was the word Mother used — I was eight when it happened — and only after Mother used the word did Father become comfortable using it, too. I realize now the gift of that word — giving Father a way to think of her after she'd left her body: as a memory, a force growing out of the soil, and rock.

We laid her under the largest oak we'd ever seen, an oak alive when Cabeza de Vaca staggered through. Mother had joked that it was fortuitous the X had landed near the edge of that bluff, as another fifty feet would have placed her at the bottom of the West Fork of the Nueces, and that thought unsettled her, as she had never learned to swim.

We realized when we drew that map that was the same thing that the original settlers who'd taken the first ownership of the land must have done: drawn an X radiating out from that tree — a giant, even then. Nature has great coincidences, but none like those of man, and it was eerie to think of those settlers, the Prades, our ancestors, of whom sadly we have no pictures, drawing a crude map and doing the precise thing we were doing a hundred and fifty years later, though for different reasons. But back then it must have been apparent to them that they were poised at the edge of something new, something untouched by whites — homesteading land given to them by the territory of Texas, which had won it from Mexico in the War for Independence — the Mexicans having been awarded it by Spain, who had (with a few cursory words and pencil strokes on a map far away) claimed it from the Indians — the Lipan Apache, and the Tonkawa (who were trying to hold onto it before the Comanche from the north stole it from them . . .).

After the map was drawn we went to look at the place, all of us, that is, except for Grandfather. It was the only time I ever saw Mother cry. She refused to lean against any of us; she preferred the support of the big tree. She drenched the ground and herself with tears, as Omar held onto one leg and I held onto the other one. Father lowered his head into Mother's long brown hair and held onto all of us. There were soft breezes then, that spring.

All my life up to that point seemed to fall away, as if over the cliff, and yet it was confusing, too, since I kept growing: being torn in two directions by the richness of life, is what it felt like — the richness of the past, the promise of the future — and always wondering, How much of me is really me? What part has been sculpted by the land, and what part by blood legacy, bloodline? What mysterious assemblage is created anew from those two intersections?

*

I had been interested in all the wild things, and had been exploring the country either on foot with Grandfather's maps, or, more often, with Grandfather himself, riding bareback with him after his stroke, for he could no longer walk, and could not speak well, though he could still see, hear, and smell. He would point out things and give me his garbled name for them, and then, when I failed to understand, he would pull out the guidebook and point to what the book said that creature, or flower, or smell, or sound was.

That next spring was the year that I was nine, and the year my mother was zero, starting over again. I understood that I should see many of the things she had seen, but that I was also obligated — for myself, as well as for her — to go out and see new things. I could feel her in me. It gave me a confidence — and again, a kind of obligation, though I would not have used such a word then — to go into those wild places, where even Grandfather, on a horse, could not go.

Each night I'd tell him, and Father, and Omar, about where I'd gone that day. "You must have been in Hell's Half Acre," my grandfather would say in that deep and hoarse *cavernous* voice, and he would remember then how thirty and forty years ago he had first gone into those places, and I would feel his spirit in me as well, and I understood how family could either fall apart, like land treated badly, or could grow ever stronger, like land treated well, like the tree Mother had leaned against that time, the tree which I sometimes sat beneath, touching it with my hand where she had last touched it, and feeling it grow. Father would look at me almost in confusion, and I knew he was seeing my mother in me, for I could feel her so strongly, too, and this curious growth and death that is a simultaneous braiding and unraveling . . .

There were always flowers on her grave, and always birds singing. There were bluebonnets and paintbrushes and phlox and primrose and prairie verbena; agarita blossoms, a few prickly pears, and the immensely rare *Styrax*, or Texas snowball. (After I went to college I was to discover that there were only sixty-six known individuals of *Styrax* in the world, and that the taxonomists did not include our population of twelve plants, in the cliffs below Mother's spot, and I did not tell them about it, then or now, though now I am a grown woman myself, without children, and someone should know: and what is family? Should I have married, should I have kept the family going? Where does it all go; back to the land? Do we only borrow it — family history, and spirit?

I was interested in all the wild things — the bobcats and mountain lions, the flowers and the trees, the rocks and the river — but the year that I was nine and my mother was zero, the year that my brother Omar was four, my father forty-four, and my mother's father seventy-two, what I became most interested in was birds: all of them. If it flew, I loved it. If it sang, I loved it.

I crawled through the thickets and old-growth oak and juniper forests of that magical land, out at the edge of West Texas, north of Uvalde, and at the edge of the hill country, where the water ran year round in the deep limestone river. You could see Mexico eighty miles off to the south. We lived on a ten-thousand-acre oasis of forest and woodland, with mountains full of blooming mountain laurel and cliffs bearing petroglyphs from five hundred years ago — rock etchings of Spaniards with guns and swords and iron helmets, horses and banners — but civilization passed through like only a thin breeze. Grandfather and father and Grandfather's old friend, Chubb, felt badly for me, all that time I was growing up, and the way they took care of me was, I knew, a testimony to how much they must have loved Mother. And of course I had eight years with her to remember — she didn't all go away. A lot of her is still here. Perhaps all. I still don't know entirely which part of her is her, and which of her is me. Sometimes I'll see or hear something with a strange kind of resonance and can only assume it is a thing, a scent or sound or sight, similar or maybe even identical to one which once touched her deeply, and I will pause, pondering the meaning of this response . . .

I'd crawl through the thickets and the woods and walk up along the ridgelines with Omar, being kind and sweet to him the way Grandfather and Chubb and Father were to me, trying to show him more than the three years he had with her.

I might as well not be coy about it. I'm forty-four years old now, and I still see and hear her in so many movements across the land here, every gust of breeze, every tumbling leaf. I still hear her more clearly, it seems, than I do myself. Are we always, all of us, a mystery to ourselves, in this manner? I may be mistaken, but I don't think any of us stand alone. Hawk-soar, and butterflies — water trickling, and especially the night sounds: owls, and fish splashing in the creek, the invisible sound of bats over the water, and the howls of the coyotes, the silence of the stars, the sound of the wind, the cool wind: both howling blue northers in the winter, and cool southerly prairie-scented night breezes coming up from Mexico in the summer, cooling the land and bathing us in blossom scents — huisache, agarita. Fireflies, drawing light it seemed (and blinking it through their bodies) as if fueled by the presence of joy, or happiness, somewhere in the world, and that energy has, and still is, on Prade Ranch . . .

I hear her more than ever, on Prade Ranch. I hear my

own blood, too, and the slight variations from her within it — my own self, scribed by the land beyond what my family's blood has scribed into me — and I am glad that I do not feel the need to fight or be uncomfortable with who I am and where I have come from.

I hear her speak to me in the night, in the special places — looking at the Nueces, or walking over the moonlit caliche roads. I do not mean to say that I hear her in the language of humans — or rather, in the English language — it's more like the echo of sound that I hear rather than sound itself; like the moment right after a word is spoken, or a door is closed. It is like the sound you hear in real life that wakes you from your dream, at the same time managing to incorporate itself into your dream.

Late at night I would take Omar with me, when all he wanted to do was play games in the library, or listen to the faraway staticky crackle of baseball games on the radio: one lone antenna rising a hundred feet into the air, up out of the river canyon, up above the great trees around our house. The antenna *strived* toward the stars, trying to pick up those mysterious night waves that would bring the games into the den every night, and Father and Omar would sit in the den with only one lamp on, as if in a trance, listening to the drone and murmur of the game; the steadiness of its slow progression punctuated infrequently by the wooden crack of a bat or the smack of ball-to-leather mitt, and the crowd's roar right after those sounds, and the announcer's excited outcry, and Father and Omar seemed to draw a kind of strength from the games, night after night.

Grandfather and I would sit on the back porch, the flat clay tiles hauled up from Mexico more than a hundred years ago, in wagon after wagon. Chubb would already be down at his cabin, drinking, or perhaps already asleep; he did not like the darkness, and retired to his cabin every day at dusk, and drank occasionally, and never ventured out before dawn.

So Grandfather and I would sit there in our own darkness and listen to the indistinguishable low sounds of the baseball game, and to the steady echo of the stars above us, and those cool breezes. The longer we sat out there, with our backs to the light, the brighter the stars got. Grandfather knew them all. Andromeda. Cassiopeia. The Pleiades. Cygnus.

We'd listen to the coyotes, to the Mormon crickets, and to the screech owls. We had an old mercury vapor lamp down on the river, below the high cliffs, to provide light for the cookouts we used to have, but did not have so often, later. There was an ancient stone gazebo down on the river, and we could see it below us, through the tops of the trees, looking strange and empty with no one sitting around it. The light brought insects to it at night, some swarming just over the water, and we could hear fish jumping at them.

We'd sit and listen to the night — would listen to it in the darkness. Fireflies drifting through the woods just beyond us, as if asking us to follow them. The giant ghostlike luna moths would fly in from out of the woods and hover at the windows, fluttering like small hawks, trying to get in to where Omar and Father were listening to baseball. The moths were a luminescent, feathery pale green with sweeping forked tails that made them look like angels in long robes. Some people said that, as with the lightning bugs, luna moths spent their days flying around the earth at high altitudes, descending only after the sun had set, but Grandfather and I knew that they lived under old logs back in the dark cedar thickets, because we'd found them in there. They didn't come from above, but emerged from the earth below. I want there to be a heaven, an afterlife, but wonder why we look to the stars so often when thinking of it. It would be just like one of nature's ironies for us to inhabit the earth, the muddy, rocky soil, in our afterlife — under logs with luna moths and lightning bugs, sleeping all day and coming out only after dark.

Already by the time I was ten I knew most of what there was to know about the night: the names of things. Occasionally Grandfather would say something I could not understand, and after a few tries he would have to write down on a notepad what he was trying to say, what he was trying to show me.

Grandfather thought it was important to know the names of things — that once the names could be spoken, knowledge would follow. He thought it was a fierce obligation of humanity to understand the names of the land as one would know the names of one's own family; brothers and sisters, aunts and uncles, mother and father. Chubb snorted at this kind of talk and said Grandfather was like an Indian that way, and Grandfather would get angry then, and would shake. And back before Mother died, back when his voice was still clear, Grandfather would shake his fist and thunder at Chubb (who loved upsetting him): "The natural history of Texas is being sacrificed upon the altar of generalization! You must pay attention! You must know the names, before they're lost!"

Chubb didn't really know what Grandfather was railing about, "the altar of generalization," but he liked to hear Grandfather say it. The way a thing is of a place — of one place, rather than all places, or no place, is what he meant, I think.

*

After the baseball game ended — nine-thirty or ten-thirty for the games in the East or in faraway Houston, but even later for West Coast games — Father would come out onto the porch and tell us good night, and Omar would, too. And if it was a school night, I'd let Omar go on to sleep. But if it was a weekend, or in the summer, I'd grab Omar before he could go off to bed, and make him come with me. I'd hug Father good night, and Grandfather, too. Grandfather would go in with Father, then — sometimes they'd talk in slow quiet voices, but more often they just sat in the near-darkness, with only a single lamp on — sitting in the darkness and just thinking, but doing it together.

Omar and I would run, then, hand in hand, through the junipers, the cedars, and out to the ghostly white of the caliche road. For a long time as I was growing up I wondered why they let us be so free. I wondered why, after such a great loss, they ever let us out of their sight. Later I realized that it was their way of fighting that loss, sitting there in the darkness and feeling, vicariously, our hearts running through the night, and through the woods — a way of speaking to the sorrow, and to Mother, too — a way of saying that all had not been for naught, that her children's lives and joy would be irrepressible, because they had come out of her.

But it would take more loss, and more years, before I saw that. All I did then was run, holding Omar's hand.

I tried to make him *feel* Mother, but I couldn't do it by talking about it: and in fact the only chance there was of him feeling and hearing her the way I did was by not talking about it. It was my job (like a frontier scout, like a map-maker) to seek out and find those edges, those vaporous places where she was each day and each night: and to stand at those edges, and listen.

I never dared talk: never opened my mouth to attempt the garbled words that would do her no good in this new life, the star life, the rock and soil life. Even then, I knew that my being alive, and running hard and fast across the earth, was the way to speak to her, and was the thing she wanted to see, wanted to hear. And I wanted Omar to see what it was about: all of it. The altar of specificity, not abstraction. The altar of the senses.

I ran with him through the dark sweet-smelling cedars to the stripe of white road, and paused, panting, letting him soak up the light of the moon, letting him *inflate* with the excitement I felt at being alive.

We'd run past the ancient headstone of someone named Father Maloney, who (said Grandfather) had been killed horribly by the Comanche, who liked to torture their enemies by pulling strips of flesh from the captive and then eating it before the victim's horrified eyes. We'd always pause at Father Maloney's old grave and wonder if, a hundred and fifty years ago, he had died that way. The woods all around his grave were silent and serene, and gave us no clue. (Sometimes at the supper table Omar and I would pretend we were Comanche; Omar would get a wild look on his face, stare across the table at me, grip the deer rib he was eating, or the chicken wing, point to me to indicate that I was to be Father Maloney, and then he would begin chewing savagely at the rib or wing, peeling back long strips of flesh and growling like a wild dog while I pretended to be in anguish, rolling my eyes and whispering *No, no,* while Omar growled and shook the rib or wing in his mouth like a dog, until Father told him to behave . . .)

We'd break our reverie at Father Maloney's marker then, and grip hands again and run. The fireflies would be moving across the meadow below, down toward the river, at the edge of the trees; we'd catch our breath and then we'd run across the moon-meadow, right through the middle of the fireflies — like running through outer space — and back into the woods, running down toward the mercury vapor lamp, and to Old Chubb's cabin.

Old Chubb always slept with his lights on. He'd come out to work on Prade Ranch even before Mother met Father: back when Mother was in high school. He'd come across from Mexico, an illegal alien, I suppose, but he'd outlasted eleven presidents and thirteen governors, and finally the governor gave him amnesty — that word! Like he was some kind of outlaw! — in 1976.

Amnesty. He always fit this country. Except for his fear of darkness, he fit this country like stamen and pistil, like the night-blooming cirrus. He dug postholes under that hard sun out in the blaze-white of the caliche flats, running fence lines all his life, not to keep cattle in, it seemed, but to keep the faraway neighbors' livestock out: working in the bright sun and the backbreaking heat with Grandfather day after day, year after year. Grandfather referred to all livestock as either "large, hoofed, chomping, stomping, shitting creatures" or "the artifacts of man." Wild pigs and sheep were the worst. We couldn't keep the pigs out — feral European wild boars — they'd go right under the fence, and no one could afford to fence ten thousand acres with the hog wire that would keep them out. So for a long time Grandfather and Chubb shot the wild pigs whenever they saw them, and chased them with hounds at night, too — but then Grandfather and Chubb got too old, and in the manner of Chubb outlasting the laws of Texas, the pigs outlasted Grandfather and Chubb. Neither Father nor Omar nor myself ever had the necessary fierceness required to kill them and so now, even though they did not evolve with the land, the pigs have assumed a place on it — a savage place, rutting up the riverbanks and destroying birds' nests, turkey and quail eggs, and other fragile things. I simply cannot bring myself to kill them, despite my love for the land. It's their sociability that always prevented me from hunting them. I knew killing them would please Grandfather, but the pigs always moved through the woods as a family, several generations of them living together sometimes. I'd throw rocks at them, or snap off a long dead cedar limb (like a javelin) and run at them, shrieking like a hawk or a lion (their only true enemies, besides Grandfather and Old Chubb), but I could never assume the responsibility for destroying a family unit. It was hard enough to shoot quail, or catch fish, or the terrible time that I shot the deer.

But the pigs harmed the land, while Chubb protected it. Doing his own kind of rooting, both he and Grandfather, slamming the heavy steel posthole diggers down into the limestone: not really battling the earth, but *engaging* themselves with it. The blows of the posthole digger sending shudders through the men's bodies, until they became one with the rhythm of the earth below, like riding a horse, or making love — for I have dug postholes in that country, too.

And then the guilty part, the part that to me never felt right, but which I knew was necessary, and which I could tell Grandfather and Old Chubb thought was the best part: stringing the wire fence from post to post, hammering the fence staples into the cedar posts and stretching the barbed wire until it was singing, the men's backs wet and the bright steel wire glittering in the sun. I knew it was necessary to protect our land, to keep it wild, and to keep the ravages of domesticity out, but the paradox of it bothered me even then: trying to put borders on a thing, in order to protect it. I wish it were all wild. I wish the wild could come and go as it pleased. I don't know why these pure wild things always seem to attract the artifacts of man, which always damage or at least dilute those clean things.

When they didn't have fence-stretchers, they would loop one end of the wire around the saddle horn and stretch it by one of them clicking the horse slowly backward (more power in the huge hind legs of those little ponies) while the other man hammered in the staples to pin the singing wire snug against the new-driven post, the green cedar accepting almost gratefully the sharp steel points of the staples. The wind then passed across the new-stretched wires, making a slightly different sound now, still inaudible to us but surely audible to the angels, and to the cardinal on her nest, to the coyotes and skunks, the lions, the beetles, the kit foxes . . .

*

Omar and I would crouch at the window and watch Old Chubb sleep. The stone walls inside his small cabin were covered with maps of places he'd been, old maps of Texas, and of the Mexican states of Sonora, Chihuahua, Durango, and Zacatecas. On these rough maps Chubb had penciled in the names of unusual sights he'd seen, and the dates the birds, or other phenomena, had been sighted. It was a treasure chest of natural history — old, barely legible pencil drawings showing Mexican wolf dens in Durango and Zacatecas, and a big wallowed-out area, a bear rub, with the words "oso grande" — almost certainly one of the last Mexican grizzlies — marked "9-4-41" . . . The common but beautiful creatures, too — the flycatchers, nuthatches, finches, jays, and vireos — they were all there, their times and places in history marked all over Chubb's gas station highway maps, curled and yellowing at the edges. When he filled up one map he left it hanging and simply taped up another one and began all over, until most of the beautiful stone wall (pre-Cambrian iron-rich) of rust red sandstone was obscured by the dry ancient parchment . . .

He had county maps on his wall, too, old maps of our own Real County. (It's pronounced like the Spanish — Ree-yowl. I like that it's pronounced that way instead of the other way, the domestic way.)

We would stare through the thin glass windows (the panes gas-bubbled and thin, distorted with age) and watch Chubb snore, sleeping like a loyal old hound, still dressed in whatever he'd been wearing that day, as if he'd never believed the day was going to end, and had been surprised by sleep . . . sleeping there still all dressed up, with only his shoes kicked off, as if trusting that one day simply rolled into the next, and that he was never going to die.

His many pairs of binoculars, hanging from wooden pegs all through his small cabin. Rusting traps hanging on the wall; he pulled them up as he found them on his walks, carried them home like a thief to a place where they could do no harm, disengaged them, and kept them with him in his sandstone tomb . . .

We were cruel, but we were only children. His cabin door was always locked — he was *terrified* of the dark — but to see him jump, we'd sometimes toss small pebbles at the windowpane.

We could see Old Chubb stiffen at the sound. We'd toss another small pebble at the glass. We could *feel* his terror. A long pause, and then another pebble, and he'd begin to quiver, again like an old dog. Slowly, he'd reach up and pull his wool blanket up over his head, and we'd toss another pebble, just to watch the form under the blanket shake. If we had called his name in a low mournful voice, I am certain that we could have turned his graying old hair shock white in an instant.

Our hearts fresh and glistening with the purity of childhood trickery, a thing like evil, but somehow not quite, we'd grasp hands again and run for the woods, farther and farther from our house. Chubb's quaking fear would always embolden Omar, and we'd run for what seemed like forever, past the hounds' cemetery, down the caliche road, through the cedars again, and then through the big oaks: through owl-call and cricket-chirp and frog-bellow, along the creek and running in the shallows, down the limestone shoals in the moonlight, running downstream, running as if we were flying.

There is no other way to explain it: we'd run until Mother was alive. It was like blowing air on a fire, bringing coals to flame. We'd run until we ignited, until we blossomed, in her presence. Something was out there — something just beyond. Something moving away from us.

And everyone else was just sleeping, back at the house, or lying there with blankets pulled over their heads.

The water was cold on our feet, our ankles. We'd shuffle, groping with our toes for the twin ruts running down the center of the flat magic shining night river. Up until the 1930s, the east fork of the Nueces is how people in this part of the country got down to Uvalde. They'd drive their horse-drawn wagons up and down the shallow river. A hundred years of iron-rimmed wagon wheels had worn ruts in the limestone, all the way to Uvalde — ninety miles — and with our toes we'd find these narrow ruts and then walk in them, holding hands across the space between them, gaining confidence and walking through water up to our knees, then: minnows and frogs skittering ahead of us, and the night music of the river riffling against the backs of our knees.

Old Chubb knew the birds in daytime, by sight and sound, but Grandfather's expertise was the night birds: screech owls, elf owls, chuck-will's-widows, bullbats, night-hawks, duck-mutterings, and heron-croaks. But he knew the daytime birds, too. He knew them all.

We'd walk barefooted down those skinny slots, as if walking (holding hands for balance) down the never-end-ing steel rails of a train track, and we'd wiggle our feet in the cool algae, and would imagine all that had come before us, until it seemed that the cloppings of horses' hooves and the iron-grinding sounds of the wagon wheels and the twisting-wood sounds of buckboard-creak were only around the next corner; and we'd keep walking, drawn by, even becoming, the river . . . and in the night, who could say we were not? It was a perfect mix of cold water and belly fire, and those physical dualities prepared me, even then — shaped me, as if in metamorphosis, for joy to miraculously blossom from pain, and life — my new life — from Mother's death.

She was gone but not absent.

The land kept shaping me, changing me, as she would have, too; and as I would have anyway, caught up in the flow of it, though somehow seeming now to move more slowly, deeply, carefully, without her.

Omar and I would walk until we realized the wagons were gone, and until I, and perhaps he, realized that it was our turn now — that the world's attention was on us, not on the past, and that there was a shining kind of urgency to *live a life,* as those behind us had lived lives: to get out of the house and go out into the bright starry night below the limestone cliffs, and to walk, and to just *live.*

All of these things were of course simply felt, rather than understood, back then. But we did them. We got out and went into the river. The night calling us to get a jump, a head start on tomorrow, the river calling us as if there were magnets in the rocks. And we listened to them, and obeyed them, though we understood nothing, then.

The water pressing against the backs of our legs, urging us downstream.

Raccoons along either shore, watching us pass: their delicate hands groping in the shallows for clear-water mussels, making soft chirring noises as we passed. The starlight in their eyes.

I always took Omar to the cliff below Mother's place. It was on the other side of the river, where the river had cut a deep curve into the high cliff, and was still a fine place to swim in the summer, cool and shady and deep . . .

There were nights when we did not feel the pull of the river so strongly, when instead it was the lure of the oaks and the cedars that drew us out, but on those nights in the river we always ended up standing beneath Mother's cliff.

I couldn't say any of it to Omar, not then. Couldn't tell him how she'd loved to quail hunt, how she'd loved to fish; how she loved to read out loud to us, how she loved to take care of things — children, horses, dogs, Father, Grandfather. I couldn't tell him any of it, when he was still so small and not yet hungry — ravenous, rather — for it. I could just stand there and hold his hand.

I am your daughter, I wanted to shout up at the cliff, and I wanted Omar to shout, too, up at the bluff, the ghostly white limestone, the wall of rock like a drive-in movie theater screen. I wanted Omar to remember, and to never forget, how much she had loved Father, had loved me, had loved him, had even loved Old Chubb. I wanted Omar to stand there in the night, in the river, and shout *I am your son:* shouting so loudly that the strength of our voices carried into the rock and that the sound waves continued through the rock, caressing and then waking her sleeping bones, our shouts joining in with and becoming part of the living rock.

The moon glittering on the waters below, the river sliding south, riffling, trickling, and sliding, millions and billions of gallons of our clear pure water being carried south, and we'd stand there in the middle of it, the water never running out . . .

Omar would blink up at the moon, or if there were no moon, at the net of stars, Draco, Betelgeuse, Centauri. He'd watch the cliff until I knew that he felt her presence still in and with us, even if he did not understand it, and I'd be satisfied then, and we'd turn and start back upstream. It was always surprising — the river's force against us, when we tried to go back upstream. Our bare feet clutched the stone bottom, searching for those wagon tracks.

We'd leave the river when our legs began to quiver, tiring against the river's upstream force; and feeling like moonwalkers, we'd hike along the shore: up into the forest then, angling the shortcut back to the house. Nighthawks thumped and fluttered in the moonlit meadows, and once again, the fireflies convened. There are so many creatures that we take for granted in our lives that will be gone, living only in our memory. I'm afraid that the next generation may not know of whales or sea turtles — that all of mankind's motors and electrical transmissions are drowning out their own undersea system of communications, their love songs, and their warning systems, their food-gathering systems. And fireflies, too, will be gone by the next century: the world is no longer rare or special enough to hold a place for a creature that conquers darkness. What was once an elaborate social mechanism as well as an escape mechanism (to a predator looking up, the firefly must have gotten lost among the stars) is now a useless extravagance, lost in a world where there is no longer much true darkness — only parking lot vapor lamps burning all night, city light washing out the fireflies' once glamorous stars, and neon outcompeting the fireflies for sheer sexual glitz . . .

But we still have a few fireflies on Prade Ranch, and back then, when I was still growing so fast and being shaped and squeezed by things, and by the absences of a thing, too, we had whole fields of fireflies, fields blooming with swirling-light-like flowers, and we ran through them so that some-times they stuck to us and then smeared in a paste against our chests, our arms and faces as we ran through the cedars again, accidentally crushing the glowing bugs against us when we tried to brush them away, or when the sweet-smelling cedar boughs whacked against us as we ran single file through those woods.

Armadillos, like so many other intruders, had moved up into this country and flourished where the cattle grazed it down — the wizened, studious, almost scholarly armadil-los out in the moonlit meadows (to escape predation by hawks and eagles, but not owls!), snuffing with their long snouts the moist bug-seething soil beneath a landscape of drying cattle dung, nosing delicately (like some old profes-sor opening a book) the waste products of rampant domes-ticity, moving patiently from cow pie to cow pie . . .

Even though we had no cows, we had armadillos. They have disproportionately large ears, like those of a kit fox or a coyote, which they use to pick up insect sounds, and be-cause of this you couldn't really sneak right up on them (despite their myopia), because they'd hear your footfalls, even if you were tiptoeing. This was unfortunate, as we loved to catch them and paint their shells.

I'd read, however, in a children's book by Fred Gipson called *Hound Dog Man,* of a way to catch them. Omar and

I would stop whenever we saw one snorting around in a meadow, and would pick up a handful of pebbles. We'd take turns tossing the pebbles near the football-shaped animal to imitate the sound of bugs jumping around in the grass. We'd toss each pebble just in front of the armadillo, keeping them just out of his reach, and in that manner lure him straight in to where we were sitting. By the time we'd lured him to within ten or fifteen feet he would have us scented, and would rear up on his hind legs and sniff and squint into the darkness. We'd stay motionless (Omar quivering, trying not to giggle), and finally the armadillo would come in close enough for one of us to snatch him up by the tail and lift him off the ground. The armadillo would twist and snort and sneeze, struggling to get free.

Some nights we'd catch two or three this way. We'd take them back to the barn (the smell of sweet alfalfa hay, trucked in from the high plains of New Mexico, smelling of high mountain air, purple skies, rich afternoon thunderstorms cleansing the hay, which then dried quickly in the thin sun ...) and with a can of phosphorus and a paintbrush, we'd paint the backs of the armadillos' shells — blow on them to dry them — and then carry them down to the deep clear-watered pool that Grandfather and Chubb had built by making a small dam below Chubb's cabin.

We'd pass his still-lit cabin, both of us carrying the armadillos in an old cedar chest, like treasure. We'd go down to the picnic grounds, set the chest down at the pool's edge, and begin dumping the glow-in-the-dark armadillos into the pool. We also painted the backs of the many large turtles that were unfortunate enough to be caught by us — painting not just designs, but also names on their backs — *Chubb, Omar, Anne* (me), *Frank* (Grandfather), *Wilson* (Father), *Lucy* (Mother) ...

Armadillos can walk underwater. We'd watch them tumble in slow motion to the depths of the pool, landing upside down on the clear limestone bottom, but always righting themselves. They'd be glowing as bright as the moon, and the turtles were, too. We didn't give it a second thought, and in retrospect, I hope that the phosphorus (which wore off after a couple of weeks, anyway) helped strengthen both the turtles' and the armadillos' shells. But it didn't matter. We were young and largely amoral and would have probably done it anyway.

Omar and I would sit at the pool's edge and watch as the lit up creatures moved slowly about, far below, each turtle and each armadillo going about its own business as if unaware that it, and the others around it, were seen by us from above, luminous . . .

*

Those were the weekends, and the summers. We'd come in well past midnight — sometimes closer to two or three in the morning — and wash our hands and our faces and go to sleep then; to sleep until midmorning (the faraway sounds of Old Chubb fooling around in the barn, up at dawn, only the faintest intrusion into our sleep, and easily absorbed by our dreams . . .).

Father and Grandfather would have fallen asleep upright in their chairs with the static of the gone-away radio station crackling between them, and we always turned the radio off before going down the dark hallway, leaving the two men sleeping there in silence.

Father worked as a county agent, traveling around the county trying to talk the other ranchers out of grazing so many cattle, and trying to get them to get rid of sheep and goats entirely, though neither of these duties fell in his job description: he was supposed to be helping them *maximize* their gains, almost always at a strain upon the land. But despite his beliefs that this country wasn't made for static livestock grazings, he was quicker than anyone to climb upon a neighbor's windmill and help replace a gasket, or to look for a lost cow, to help out in any way he could; and we were as poor as any of them, with each year a struggle to pay the taxes just to continue living upon the land. We ate roast pig and venison and duck and wild turkey and fish, and Old Chubb worked the two-acre garden in the early mornings with the doves cooing, and again in the late afternoons when the doves began to mourn again, and each year, the rules of the government came close but could never quite foreclose upon our wildness: there was each year, always and barely, enough for taxes.

Mornings were better than evenings, for Father and Grandfather. Father always made us breakfast: fresh eggs that he had traded for (he and Grandfather both despised the sound and smell of chickens, though Grandfather was not above staking one out in a field to try to lure in a hungry hawk or eagle he wanted to watch).

Grandfather and Omar and I would sit out on the cool tiles on the back porch and watch Old Chubb out in the garden. Grandfather would ask, in his odd assemblage of sounds, where we'd gone last night — the word "where" the only one we could even remotely understand, but we knew what he was asking.

With the end of a stick, I'd sketch in the dust a map of where we'd gone, as I told him about it: what we'd seen and what it had been like. I told him all but the unspoken part, but I think he understood that, too.

He'd nod vigorously as I sketched each bend in the river, and individual trees, individual boulders; he'd make satisfied groans and croaking noises, and the wilder the places were that we'd visited the night before, the more excitedly he'd nod. He'd been there. He knew everything. Surely he could hear her, could see her, too.

Father would call us to breakfast. We'd wolf the food down, and then Father would walk out into the bright sunlight, to the old car the county provided him, his soil-testing kit in the back seat (it would always tell him what he already knew: that the surrounding lands were being overgrazed and were overly saline from pumping out too much ground water), and a box of lettuce and potatoes and sweet onions in the trunk from our garden, for whoever wanted any.

Omar and I would walk up to the county road and wait for the school bus, or if it was summer or a weekend — one of those long lazy mornings, with a late breakfast — we'd return to the cool tiles of the back porch, would lie there in the shade and watch Chubb working in the glittering green garden, wearing one of his same old two pair of denim overalls. Brown face. Straw hat. Sweat rolling down his face. The scratching sound of the tiny hoe in the big earth. We'd just lie there in the half-grogged morning sleepiness of childhood and watch him, the way the night before the raccoons had watched us make our way down the river.

I am increasingly unsure of the division we put between the past and the present. It seems, the more time I spend wandering the land, seeing the things my parents saw, and feeling the same things, almost as if I am, at times, them — as if our biological progress has been so infinitesimal that there's no significant difference between us — that there is no true fence, no stone wall, between the present and the past: that we construct (out of fear, or hunger for the future, *gluttony*, these fences behind us; that we turn our backs on who and what we really are — who and what we still are.

It seems a form of disrespect.

I love the past so much because I love the present. I know I have to go into the world and become shaped, altered, bent, myself — *individuated* — and that there will be pain and joy in the process. I am not the land itself, neither am I a clone of my family. But the magnitude of my attachment to these things — and the stability it affords — staggers me. What strengthens or protects these things strengthens and protects me; that which harms them, harms me. There is still a connection to these things here on Prade Ranch.

*

I wasn't much of a social creature. I made average grades in school, and devoured the sciences, but I didn't have a lot of friends in school, or growing up. Mostly it was Omar, and Father and Grandfather, and Chubb, and the woods.

It is true I was too serious. But perhaps the other children, and even the teachers, were not serious enough. The spider's silk lines of chance that can break and wash out from beneath you one or more of your cornerstones, toppling you into heartache and confusion, estrangement. Perhaps I was too aware of the tenuousness (and hence the beauty) of one's foundations, but I often thought others around me were not enough aware.

*

I love the wild things, and the birds most of all. My education began, I am sure, the moment I was pushed free of the womb by Mother, born on Prade Ranch in the back bedroom on a late afternoon in early March — the seventh of March, which is when the golden-cheeked warblers usually return to Prade Ranch after wintering down in Mexico. There would have been doves calling, as if to counter Mother's gasps and cries, and the flylike buzz of the hummingbirds (the aggressive black-chinned ones making most of the racket) at the nectar feeders just outside the open window. There would have been a breeze stirring the lace curtains. Father in the room with the doctor, and Grandfather and Chubb on the back porch, waiting for this next new part of the world to begin. Grandfather said he knew that was going to be the day, not just because of the golden-cheeked warblers' return, but because he'd heard a vermilion flycatcher buzzing — *pit-zee, pit-zee* — all the day before, and on into the night, well past midnight — the only time he's ever heard that, before or since.

Grandfather said that as I was being born, a broad-billed hummingbird flew up on the porch and rested on the dinner bell — Grandfather timed it — unmoving for thirty minutes, just sitting there and cocking its head occasionally, waiting, while all the other hummingbirds swarmed the feeder.

By nightfall, I was in my mother's arms.

Certainly the land impressed itself upon me, as I was carried and then walked across it, learning — imprinting — Prade Ranch's various slants of light, the sound of Grandfather's snores, the constant murmurs and splashings of the East Fork, and the birdsongs, the teeming bird cries that became, each spring, a symphony. All of these became my *home*, my rules and systems, the borders within which I lived, and to do harm to or take any one of them away would have fragmented part of my self. And it occurred to me by the time I was a teenager that I had become part of the land, every bit as much a part of it as sparrow eggs or thrasher nest, garter snake or oak tree, and that the rest of my life, or anyone's life, would be a gradual learning process, a journey toward fitting into one's home, for those of us lucky enough to still recognize what is home . . . that which we are a part of, rather than estranged from. And rather than using the word "lucky," perhaps I should use the word grace.

They were all four good teachers: Grandfather, Father, Mother, and Chubb. I suppose I take after Grandfather the most, with regard to being in the woods. One of my first memories is of when I was three or four years old, playing on the back porch in the twilight while the grown-ups finished supper. Chubb was eager to get back to his cabin before true dark, and was trying to say his good-nights. My mother and father were moving slower, however, sitting back in the darkness and watching the dusk come in, listening to the birds and sipping margaritas. They were both dressed in white that day, and back in the dimness then, and in the dimness of memory now, I could just see their shapes, not their faces. But I remember the moment.

A nighthawk had flown into the yard and was leaping about in the grass, flushing and then chasing insects, not thirty feet away from us. In future years, while out walking in winter, Omar and I would sometimes find nighthawks huddled in a hole in the ground as cold as an ice cube, in a state not unlike hibernation, called torpor, where their body temperature lowers to whatever the surrounding temperature is. We'd carry them home (their huge dark luminous night-eyes wet and unblinking, believing, perhaps, that it was all only a dream). Again, amoral — but wild — Omar and I would warm the birds in the oven at 125 degrees, until they slowly came back to life. We'd watch them through the glass door of the oven, and when they began to stir, we'd open the oven door and let them fly out, circling the kitchen once or twice before heading out the open door and back into the cold, where they would promptly "hibernate" again, for there were no insects out in such weather, and it would have been a waste of their energy, and their life, to look for a thing that was not there . . .

But this time that I am remembering — my first conscious memory — is from before the arrival of Omar. We were on the back porch watching this nighthawk chase moths, and Chubb was fidgeting, anxious to get back to his cabin before the light was gone.

I don't remember the words, but the import of what was happening was that Chubb believed that all nighthawks were "goatsuckers" — that they flitted low to the ground like that, right at dusk, trying to come up out of the grass and suck on the udders of all the animals in the woods — not just the goats, cows, and sheep on the surrounding ranches, but the deer in our woods. Grandfather said this was ridiculous, miffed that Chubb would believe such an old wives' tale. Chubb said that he always saw the nighthawks hovering under the bellies of animals at dusk, that he had seen them suck, and that the next day the animal's milk had been dry — sucked out.

It was a big argument. Why the two men — the closest of friends — would argue so vehemently, I couldn't understand, though I realize now that birds were their passion, and that when passion's involved . . .

I could hear the nighthawk's soft tremulous whirring as it flounced through the tall grass. I tried to concentrate on that, rather than on the two men arguing. Mother and Father said nothing: staying back in the darkness, sipping those drinks. Fireflies.

Grandfather was sputtering. He said that the nighthawks were chasing the bugs that swarmed the sweaty beasts, and that in the failing light that nighthawks like to hunt in, it just appeared that they were suckling the livestock. Grandfather said that what Chubb must have seen, and what all the "previous generations of blind, inattentive, head-bobbing myth-mongers," before Chubb (I'm imagining this now, knowing Grandfather) must have seen was nighthawks pecking insects off of the animal's hide, so that it would have looked like the nighthawks were nursing. And that if the udders did occasionally dry up the next day, it was from the fright of being swarmed by the nighthawks, or maybe even by being pecked by one.

Chubb was insistent, however. Nothing less than his entire culture was at stake — goatsuckers is what they were called in Mexico, and in deep South Texas, and goatsuckers is what they were.

And nothing less was at stake for Grandfather — his crusty belief in anarchy, his certainty that everyone was lazy, that no one thought things out for themselves anymore, that the world was going to hell in a hand basket, and it was because of a loss of attention to detail, a lapse in our glorious God-given ability to *observe*.

I thought the two men were going to strike each other —

each was so angry at, and disappointed with, the other —
each shocked by and convinced of this stupendous flaw
they'd discovered in each other simultaneously, and feeling
tricked, feeling let down . . .

Fireflies began to blink out in the yard as never before.
A great horned owl began to boom down on the creek —
by Chubb's cabin — and more nighthawks, or goatsuckers,
appeared in the yard, swarming among the hundreds, perhaps thousands of fireflies, like huge bats, while those
nighthawks that were still hidden in the grass below continued to chirr their eerie, drifting, murmuring calls that
were impossible to locate, calls which seemed to be coming
from everywhere.

"A hawk don't drink *milk*," Grandfather would have
said, talking the way he did when he was angry. And then
Chubb would have said, one more time, but less insistently
— his culture, his identity! — *"Goatsucker."*

I remember thinking they were going to scuffle. And I
remember feeling Chubb's terror at being stranded there on
the porch, at being surrounded by the dark, and robbed of
his identity as well, as the truth of what Grandfather was
saying — the *possibility* of it — began to sink in. I could
feel Chubb, hot as an oven, standing next to me.

It was a dark like I have never seen — full of the swirling
green tracer-flights of fireflies, and echoing with the strange
calls of the great horned owl and the everywhere wavering
ghostly calls of the nighthawks. I remember that Grandfather did not strike Chubb, then, but did something far
worse: he said, "Go on, then, run, you big ninny," and
there was nothing for Chubb to do but run, giving a short
yelp as he jumped down off the porch and ran through the
night, through the lightning bugs, running for the light of
his cabin, but running toward the terrible sound of the
great owl, which, for all he knew, was resting on the eave
above his front door, waiting for him. Chubb yelped and
cried out as he ran — surprising the nighthawks resting in

the grass, which leapt up and brushed their feathers against him — and I heard Grandfather roar, "Go on, you lily, *run*, the goatsuckers are after you!" and then I heard the door to Chubb's cabin slam, and there was nothing but the continued soft peents of nighthawks, sounding subdued now, and Grandfather's heavy breathing, as if he'd been the one doing the running, and an odd, frightening silence there on the porch then, a kind of confusion, with no one saying anything, and everyone bothered by something, and I stood on the edge of consciousness, of complexity and paradox, and after a while the owl began to hoot again, and the summer katydids and tree frogs began to sing.

It must have been tough for my Grandfather to have lived when he did, in between the wild and the tame — to have seen regularly wolves, lions, and bears in this country, and then to see nothing — to have so much taken away. I don't hold him accountable for his moments of rough wildness or cruelty, which were rare and always far apart. In light of what the world had brought him, it seems that perhaps he could have used even more rough wildness than that which was already in him. That even, rough as he was, he was still too tender. I hope my own core will, through time, become strengthened to be at least as durable as his.

And if his roughness were a thing that needed forgiving — if there somehow were anyone in a moral position of being able to judge his roughness-in-the-world — I think they would have to remember and balance his tenderness, too.

There are none among us who have not been, even for a moment, cruel to those whom we love most, as if unable, in that moment, to shoulder any longer the magnificent weight and burden, the responsibility, of that love.

In the morning Grandfather took me with him when he took coffee down to Chubb, and they sat on his porch and drank it and watched the red-winged blackbirds screech and whistle in the windblown cattails along the creek while

I played in the dust. I don't know what was said. I remember feeling like everything was all right again. I remember a breeze in the tops of the trees. And I have never heard anyone in our family mention, or even acknowledge, the presence of nighthawks ever since, save Omar and me. This was a forgotten memory, one which the land resummoned in me only recently, on a walk along Panther Creek, and I shudder now to think of the discomfort it must have caused Chubb, Grandfather, and my mother and father a few years later, to see Omar and me carrying those winter-chilled nighthawks in from out of the fields. Those innocent, trusting, sleeping nightbirds.

Those goatsuckers.

*

Before Mother returned to the earth, before we chiseled the limestone resting spot six feet deep beneath the big oak — before Grandfather lost his voice, and before I set about trying to show Omar where she could still be found, and teaching or showing him the history of her, which he had missed, by being too young — for Grandfather was mute for history, now, and Father was numbed to history, no longer able to bear its weight — even before all that, it was simple: I would go into the woods with Grandfather, and sometimes with both Grandfather and Chubb, and would study the birds.

By the age of five I could distinguish a lone coal black zone-tailed hawk from the flock of vultures it drifted with. I did not understand evolution then, how it benefited the zone-tailed hawk to mimic the vultures, drifting with them, but different, on the high thermals above the river canyon. The only big difference was that the zone-tail had yellow legs, so that it could identify itself to both the vultures and to other zone-tails, for mating purposes: but to the wary rodents below, who were color-blind, when they looked up at the sky, at the shadows that had passed in front of the sun, all they saw was a flock of vultures circling overhead, looking for something dead, not living.

The rabbit, or squirrel, would look away, relieved, believing that it was vultures, not hawks.

And then the one zone-tail, this tremendous bird, would fold its wings and dive, would fall out of the vultures' formation in a stoop like that of a peregrine, only so much larger and more terrible, screaming silently toward the earth, toward the small mammal below, like a chunk of black iron, the vulture that was not a vulture, while above, the vultures continued to circle, as if pretending that nothing had ever happened.

Pulling up out of its stoop at the last second, and swinging those yellow legs, those curved talons (like a bear's) out from underneath the feathered plummet: this *locomotive* falling from the sky, the talons striking hard across the animal's back with a force that usually snapped the spine instantly, and knocked the animal head over heels across the dust, into a clump of trees. (If the zone-tail's talons got locked into the animal's body, the zone-tail would go rolling along with its intended as well, and was sometimes injured, even killed, in that manner.)

We try and map the boundaries, and to string fence — we try to set up a border between life and death, between man and nature, and complicity versus innocence. But the truth is, there is no complicity, there is no innocence; and there is no death, there is only life. We're all interrelated: we're all one organism — hawk and rabbit, daughter and mother. After the kill, the zone-tail would hop over to his betrothed (warm blood trickling from the rabbit's nose) and begin tearing at the fur. Tufts of the fur would be carried away on the river breeze like cottonwood fluff in the fall. The hawk would then begin pulling the bright-colored entrails out: would seize them in its beak and begin hopping backward, as if unraveling its prey.

All of this duly noted by the vultures above, who witnessed, and perhaps even gave counsel to the scene: descending, a day later, to eat that which the hawk had been unable to finish.

The price of life; the price of inclusion in life! *There are no boundaries.* It is all wrapped up together, all hawk-and-boar tumble, and if God does not take us out by the hawk, we will be eaten by the vultures. Had my mother lived, I think I would have been cast in one direction. In her death, I have probably been cast in another, though who can say for sure? I know our bloodlines shape us at least as strongly as does the land itself, and it is of some comfort to me to realize that even in her absence she has helped direct and shape me, as if still living — though strangely, I suspect, in a direction somewhat different from the path I would have taken had she lived. We bend and flex, and are altered, or alter ourselves. A kind of motion accrues, like the movement of a snake across sand. We find that we are changing and gaining direction whether we plan that direction or not.

Grandfather and Chubb and I would hide motionless in the brush and watch the vultures, would watch as a zone-tail drifted in to join them, and we could detect, from slight behavioral differences, a certain alienation between the zone-tail and the vultures; but they accommodated one another, acknowledged the sheer uncontrollability of borders, and used that freedom to the best of nature's imagination.

Nature's imagination. While my classmates were lying in front of the television watching commercials, I was watching a zone-tail drop from the sky (those splendid yellow legs, the telltale giveaway, tucked, hidden within the recesses of shiny, vulture-like, greasy black feathers) to strike the lead turkey in a flock of young poults not twenty yards away from where we were hiding . . .

An explosion of iridescent copper and green and bronze and blue feathers, turkey feathers, turkey down, floating all around us as if there'd been a pillow fight, turkey feathers floating downwind, following the river's breezes to Uvalde, and like a thief, Old Chubb ran out and stripped a piece of breast meat from the dead turkey (the rest of the stunned flock pausing a good ten seconds before scattering). The zone-tail shrieked its anger at Old Chubb, but he got away, and like pirates, the three of us shared that breast meat for supper that night with Grandfather saying a prayer first, like an Indian, thanking the zone-tail for "the bounty that is this life . . ."

*

So many of my childhood memories involve a force from the sky, the silent approach of beautiful strength, beautiful speed. There are two old pear trees in front of the house, trees that were root-planted by Mother's grandfather in the fall of the first year of this century. For decades those two trees have been making sweet pears, and one day as Mother and I were watching a squirrel go from branch to branch gathering the pears (dropping them to the ground, and having to start all over), Mother said, "He'd better watch out in the broad daylight like this — a hawk is going to get him" — and I scanned the blue sky but saw nothing, but five seconds later a red-tailed hawk came sailing through the pear tree and grabbed the squirrel on the fly. Into our lives, and then out, with the squirrel hanging limply from his talons. Strong wingbeats. Those two pear trees were sixty years old then, and only now, as they approach one hundred, are they beginning to slow down in their sweet-blossomed, profligate ways. The bounty. The squirrel was gone, just like that: eating pears in one instant, being carried over the horizon in the next. "Speak of the devil," my mother had said with satisfaction, for although she loved squirrels, she also loved pears and hawks, and above all, small miracles, small secrets.

Yet another time, when I was seven or so — Omar was in the world, but not yet old enough to go out into the woods — I was down along the river with Grandfather and Chubb. I had been reading bird books and had developed a crush that week on peregrine falcons, noting on the bird index's map that once we had been right on the edge of their distribution, but that the poisoning programs for rodents and coyotes, and the insecticides sprayed on the land, had all but exterminated them from the area. But the book said they liked river cliffs, and we certainly had such cliffs.

We were standing on the sandbar beneath the magic spot — the high chalky cliff where Mother would be buried in a year. We were watching swallows through the binoculars. It was one of the few mistakes I ever saw Grandfather make in science, and it was not really so much a mistake as it was bad timing.

"Are there any peregrines left out here?" I asked the two men, and Grandfather, angry at the beautiful birds' loss, I think, growled, "Hell, no, I've never seen one out here in all my days, and believe me, if one was here, I'd have seen it" — and not three seconds had passed when Chubb pointed to the flock of swallows just as a peregrine falcon ripped into them, vaporizing its beloved prey, its lone intended, into a powder of feathers. I think that this almost made up to Chubb for the time about the nighthawk, and I think it was good for Grandfather too — that it reminded him (to never forget again) that the heart of it all is mystery, and that science is at best only the peripheral trappings to that mystery — a ragged barbed-wire fence through which mystery travels, back and forth, unencumbered by anything so frail as man's knowledge.

The thing about nature is that each species does what it's best at. That's why it's all so locked together. I'm certain that at its center is some kind of peace or unity or harmony — the white light people speak of having seen when they come back from "the dead." And what does our species do best? We construct artificial systems wherein we are mighty predators, or mighty *thinkers,* or sagacious, benevolent rulers of the universe — allies with God, even — but I have spent my life (as has my family before me) outside of those artificial systems. I have spent my life in the brush — and I have seen what it is we do best, and that is to love and honor one another: to love family, and to love friends, and to love the short days. We are only peripheral trappings ourselves, on the outside of the mystery. We are songbirds.

As I see the lands outside this island of the Prade Ranch change and disappear, I want to dive deeper. Whether it's cowardly or not, or heroic or not, I don't know; all I can say for sure is that it's *true:* I want more and more to go into the deep harbor of the woods, the constancy of the woods, and of my family's history: to use these things as a source of strength to take with me, in my own changes, as I move into the future, bending, changing.

Is this how it is for a species that senses it is going extinct? Is there a feeling of loneliness, or unease, each morning, upon awakening?

*

Crawling through the cedars — intent upon knowing every square foot of this place, the way Grandfather did, and knowing full well it would take me all of my life, as it did him — crawling through the agarita, the mesquite, the mountain juniper, and the oak jungles — I saw firsthand what Grandfather had told me about niches, that everything has its place in the world, that it was all wired, in his words, "tighter than a tick," that it was all "a goddam glorious functioning miracle, a goddam *triumph.*"

The endangered golden-cheeked warblers coming up from Mexico every March, and nesting only in the old-growth cedars, because once cedars get big, their bark begins to peel off in shaggy strips, like long, sweet-smelling feathers. Building their nests in the forks and crotches of these stout old trees. Everyone knows an old cedar forest is thicker and cooler and stiller than any other kind. Birdsong carries clearer in there. It's a symphony back in there, even in the middle of the day.

The *niches* Grandfather spoke of — I saw them. The warblers nesting in tree forks at least three feet above the ground, where their vivid bursts of song can travel best, and where they can be seen by one another, in their golden brilliance, even among all the camouflage.

And below that three-foot level reside the vireos — the black-capped vireo and the zebra-looking black-and-white warbler. They lay only a few eggs on the precarious lower branches. Deer and other lithe mammals rarely bump into the nests, rarely even see them, but the bruising cloddish ways of livestock — cows staggering through the cedars where they don't belong in the first place — it should be bison, out on the grasslands, but that is another story — and the bark-stripping all-consuming ways of goats — have conspired to knock vireo eggs from their nests; but a niche is a niche, and still these brave little zebra birds go about their lives with integrity, flying to the very tops of trees to sing and mate, but living down at the very lowest level of the old-growth junipers, so that in my crawling travels I would often come face to face with the bright eyes of a mother vireo on her nest, and I would back away, would crawl off in another direction . . .

These are rare birds! I didn't know how rare they were when I was growing up. I didn't understand that we were an island of wildness, and that the very soul of the earth resided beneath our feet, and among the cedar boughs, and in our lungs. I didn't understand then that the wilderness clung to us, depended on us.

I thought I could crawl forever, and never run out of mystery, never leave the marvel. I felt like I was on fire, aflame with hunger, and I had to know it all, learn it all.

Father knew all the roads in the county, all the back lanes and farms and ranches, where everybody lived and what they did — but Grandfather, and to a lesser degree, Old Chubb, knew every inch of a much smaller place. They knew the individual trees where the birds nested, year after year. They knew individual stones, individual animals. Although my father loved the land, he loved it in a pastoral way, a gentle way.

I wanted to love it in the fierce way, like Grandfather and Chubb, who knew everything about a small ten-thousand-acre island, and who were fluent in the language of birds.

*

Some days I feel unassailable. The warblers are endangered, the vireos are declining; the jaguar is gone, and the wolf and the buffalo; Grandfather is gone, as is Old Chubb. Father lives in Fredericksburg, no longer able to bear the bigness of the country alone, and even Omar is gone, up north, way north, like some storm-tossed petrel. Only Mother and I remain. The garden has gone wild. The radio has remained silent since the day Father left. Trumpet vine has swarmed Old Chubb's stone cabin, so much so that you couldn't get in through the door, now; hummingbirds swarm it, in the early summer, delighting in the stone house's nectar. All his old maps are still tacked to the walls inside, though his ever-present glowing light bulb has long since burned out.

When I say that only Mother and I remain, I do not mean that she remains unchanging, frozen in sweet time in her limestone cave, suspended in her paused youth, her gentle grace. She's changing ... she's growing, too. She turns with the earth. She is still learning things. Some nights she circles back past our empty house, comes very close. And I still walk in the Nueces some nights, my bare feet feeling for the old wagon grooves, though not as often as I did as a child, when I was trying so desperately, without saying it, to show Omar that she was still here.

The call of a mourning dove can still surprise her at dawn. The fluttering of a poorwill still makes her turn her head.

I remember a gentle day in the early spring on the back porch, with everyone else in town. Mother and I were mending clothes. For some reason we had not yet put our feeders out, but the hummingbirds came to visit that day anyway, a flock of them, blue-throated and the exquisitely rare Costa hummingbirds — a long, long way from home. We were mending, among other things, Chubb's faded red workshirt and Omar's bright red trousers, and the little hummingbirds swarmed us. The Costas were an easy five hundred miles off course: and how could they have known we would be mending and knitting red that morning?

The blue-throateds hovered, too, watching us work. The color on their throat was exactly the color of the sky they had flown through to get here. They buzzed all around us, humming, and when I say I feel unassailable it is a feeling like the one I had that day, the notion that the hummingbirds had unseen threads in their long needle-like bills, and were flying around and around us, tying my Mother and I, my family and I, up with invisible silky grace, tighter and tighter, until our history, our past, is protected forever.

*

Chubb, out in the garden, wavy-looking in the summer's shimmering heat, so that he seemed to be half-man and half-tree, growing up out of the rich hoe-furrowed earth. Grandfather taking him a thermos of ice water: walking out across those furrows until his legs also disappeared in the heat waves, and he too seemed to become half-man and half-tree.

*

To see the songbirds, Grandfather would imitate the daytime sound of a screech owl, their mortal enemy. I would crouch in the cedars with him with my binoculars and watch as he cupped his hands to his mouth and made the ghostly, feathery *whirring* sound deep in his throat, a sound like that of the bird itself taking flight. Every bird in the woods would begin to scold us, would gather as a force and come flying toward us from all directions, seeking to harass Grandfather, the screech owl. Colored birds swarmed around us like bits of bright cloth thrown to the wind — like glitter, like dreams.

*

Chubb had a 1949 black Cadillac, which we all used to ride to Mexico in, once every several months. (After the car stopped running and our family began to disintegrate, Chubb still held on to the car: kept it propped up on blocks outside his cabin, and washed and waxed it every few weeks, even as birds and dirt daubers built nests in the engine and mice invaded the upholstery — washing it even after he was too old to carry a bucket of water up from the river, keeping the exterior bright and shiny even as the tires rotted off, even after the bobcat had her kittens in the back seat — Chubb washing it, as if believing that by keeping up its outward appearance, the rods and rings and pistons and valves and ten thousand other invisible little parts, little marvels, might someday decide to heal themselves and function once again . . .)

But back when it was running, we'd pile in and drop the top — Grandfather in front, and Mother and Father and me, and later Omar, in the back. We'd rumble down the back roads without a map, and sometimes we wouldn't even stick to the roads, but would turn down dry washes, empty or barely trickling creek beds, and in this huge glossy black rumbling high-finned goggle-eyed *witch* of a car, we'd belly-drag and frame-skid our way to Mexico, sometimes just driving across wide open country, a plume of dust behind us for miles.

When we came to a fence, Father usually knew whose fence it was, and where a gate or gap might be, and even where the key was hidden — "Under the white stone beneath the third fence post on the left," he'd instruct me, and I'd leap out and go open the gate, and then always close it behind me, after the coal black rocket ship of a car had nosed on through — and in that manner, on our trips to Mexico, we'd come down out of the wild blue mountains and strike out across the desert, stopping for a picnic or to patch a flat tire, and then making our border crossing over the bridge at Del Rio.

And although my father and mother were not big drinkers, they would always stop at some cantina, farther into Mexico, and would sit with Grandfather and Chubb and sip a margarita or two, *prudence*, while Grandfather and Chubb tossed the margaritas down, wild, until even I could see that their whole bodies were aflame, lit as bright as candles, and I would play out in front of the cantina, would sit on the wooden porch and read or play with dolls or just look out at the hot buzzing sky, and the shimmering heat of the prairie, surrounded by hummingbirds that whirred all around me, and I'd feel my skin beginning to parch, would think about the cool clear depths of the Nueces, and would go back inside and ask for a glass of water . . .

We'd stay that first night with Chubb's parents and brothers and sisters, a huge extended family of perhaps twenty or more. Chubb would bring them some money each time, and the back of the Cadillac would be loaded with venison, beef, corn, peas, and heads of lettuce — whatever bounty the Prade Ranch county had been supplying us, at that time of year — and there was the smell of flour tortillas frying dry on the woodstove, the sound of chickens, and I'd play with children I saw only a few times each year, and whose language I could barely speak, but whose names I will remember to the grave: *Ramon, Estrella, Maria, Cristobal* ... I was a stranger, an outsider, a mountain girl having come in over their border, having come in from out of the wild, and they accepted me without ever being able to speak my language ...

In the morning we would pile in the Cadillac and turn west, heading through the agricultural villages, and into the true country. Chubb was navigating now, and for all we knew we might not have been a day's journey from home, but ten thousand days', or a lifetime. What we were looking for ostensibly was painted buntings, but I knew even then — for I could feel the excitement, the candle-flame of it myself, too — that it was also nothing but a reason to get out and stretch, to migrate to new country — to drink a cold beer in the hot sun, to see new things, to get lost, to shrug off domesticity and the numbness of the predictable, the numbness of knowledge ...

All of the little villages throughout Mexico sold painted buntings back then, incredibly vivid songbirds that Audubon called our most colorful North American bird. The men in Mexico trapped them, keeping the vivid males and releasing the lemon-lime females. They kept the males in little wire cages to take to the cities and sell, not so much for the males' year-round songs (a pleasant warbling whistle alternating single- and double-phrases with watery trills), but for the sheer turn-your-head color: a bold blue head, a blood red underside, and, like a dinner jacket, an emerald green coat over the back and wings. Not a speck of white or even brown anywhere on the bird: all exploding, brilliant color.

We'd buy these lonely panting birds in their wire cages for pennies — birds and cages together. We'd stack the cages in the huge trunk of Chubb's Cadillac and take off for the next village, jouncing down the rutted roads. We'd drive until the trunk was full, and then camp by a little stream or river. We'd let the birds go, one at a time, and then throw the cages in the river, where, I imagine, fish now live in them. Grandfather wanted to band some of the buntings to see if they ever turned up at Prade Ranch, but Chubb said that they were too beautiful to band. I'll bet that over the years we must have thrown a thousand cages into that river.

Mother and Father lying in the grass on a blanket, listening to coyotes, and watching two grown men and a child release those brilliant birds. Throwing the tinny cages into the water then, like throwing rice at a wedding.

*

One of the best things my father ever did for this county, other than protecting the Prade Ranch, was to work against the Catfish Man. Grandfather wanted to go down to Bexar County where the Catfish Man lived and "knock some living sense into him" — and if that didn't work, wanted to "pull his heart out from between his ribs and eat it, right there in front of him" — but Father said that there would be unacceptable complications to either of those two solutions, and that "legal or political recourse might be more effective." Whenever Father talked that way, Grandfather would just look at him for a moment and then would stare at Mother, quite obviously trying to see what she saw in him, and wondering where he'd raised her wrong, wondering why she hadn't married someone like himself ... Mother would just laugh and Father would smile too, knowing he wasn't like Grandfather, but that it didn't matter, that he, Father, was lucky in that he could be any way he wanted to be and Mother would still love him. (His head in her lap, down there in Mexico by the river, lying on the picnic blanket while red-winged blackbirds trilled in the cattails and the world slipped away ...)

Water, of course, is why the birds are here, why everything is here in this magical spot, this seam of natural history where all the borders come together: where the Texas Oak–Juniper Hill County has its final mountainous fling, where the Chihuahuan desert from the West finally ends, where the Gulf Coastal Plain begins, stretching far to the south, to Mexico, and all the way to the ocean — and where the Great Plains, coming down from the north, also finally end. We have eight times the diversity of other places in the West because we are at the edge of all four of those zones. Unlike any other place on earth, perhaps, this is where it all comes together.

What the Catfish Man was doing was stealing water from our county — from Father's county. I mean only to speak of my natural history, and of the natural history of Prade Ranch, not the natural history of man in the West. But a little background is necessary. And unlike anyone else in our family (except perhaps now for Omar the lawyer — Omar in Philadelphia), Father was the only one who could live among the natural history of the birds — the pipits and the cranes, the owls and the oaks — and yet also move comfortably among the unnatural ways of man.

Perhaps, back in the woods, the wild things think, or sense, or believe that there are still a few sanctuaries, a few harbors, where they can stay insulated from the ways of man. And Prade Ranch would have to be one of those places. But in 1958, the dry year, Father noticed that people's springs were running dry, where they had never before paused in their ability to yield water, and that even the gorgeous green shimmering depths of the Nueces had dropped several inches, leaving crusty brown algal fuzz on the cliff walls. Some of the shoals in the river shone bone white, like the bleached hip of an old skeleton-cow's pelvis.

The mystery of life beneath this land (in the manner that I believe my mother is the mystery of life above it), is an underground river, the Edwards Aquifer, two hundred

miles long and twenty-five miles wide. It's not just intersti-
tial water locked in pore spaces, like other aquifers; this
aquifer is a river. It *flows*.

It passes beneath this land, below our feet, giving rise to
the grand carnival of life, to the secrets of things (the great
oaks' roots reach the deepest, striving to be tickled by the
river, but even the shallow grasses and flowers are nour-
ished by it). But because it is an underground river, flowing
south, it continues to the edge of what is called the Edwards Plateau, to where the plateau ends in a fault line running through the middle of the state — a fault line called
the Balcones Escarpment.

The cities lie along the Escarpment — most notably,
Austin and San Antonio. Millions of people use that water,
and they don't give it back. Even in 1959, we were running
out of water up here, because of increased usage in the faraway cities. But because it was all happening underground,
no one could understand it, or even believed it. Certainly
the politicians didn't. In 1959, Father was the only one who
understood. He made dozens of long trips to San Antonio
and Austin to meet with the county commissioners, trying
to get them to regulate the water's usage.

"You're taking away our water," he'd tell them tactfully,
but bluntly. "You don't understand: we're all hooked together. It's all related."

How they must have hooted at him, at this *clodhopper,*
this county agent who had come from a hundred miles out
in the country, out from the *desert,* to tell them they were
taking *his* water!

"Your pumpage exceeds recharge," he'd explain, laying
out a map of where he perceived the underground river
was, based on natural artesian water wells in his, and
surrounding counties — mysterious, perhaps holy places
where cold clear water gushed up out of the earth, out of
caves, and out of seams between rock formations — indi-

cating that some mysterious force was rushing past, rushing just beneath the surface, and rushing south, downdip.

I am sure that those commissioners, and those assistants-to-the-commissioners, intent only on getting the most, the absolute most they could get out of the land before checking into the sweet hereafter, called him a hayseed, a bumpkin, a hobbledehoy. I'm sure they accused his Real County neighbors — *Krauts and wetbacks,* I could hear them saying, *ignorant Krauts and wetbacks* — of running too many cattle, and drilling too many wells. And there were too many cattle. But there were too many people, too — hundreds of thousands, and then millions — and they were using a million times more water than were the cattle, or the ranchers up in the hills.

For years, Father made trips to the cities, long trips on bad roads. He'd be gone two and three days at a time. Those days added up. We cannot get them back. Mother cannot get them back, nor can Omar or I. They are gone, like a leaf or a feather carried along on a river.

*

The Catfish Man owned four acres on the hot glaring chalky outskirts of San Antonio. Father had to drive right past there on the way to his meetings in San Antonio. The Catfish Man lived alone, having fled his wife and six children in Louisiana. He had the look of an outlaw to him, always stubble-bearded and wild-haired, but Father said that he did not have the moral energy to even be an outlaw, that he was just lazy, was all.

The Catfish Man had been drilling a water well not long after he bought his four acres, intending to start a roadside auto junkyard, but struck an artesian well before he'd drilled thirty feet. The force of it blew the drillstem back out of the hole and toppled the jack-mounted truck doing the drilling.

The water flowed and flowed, for a couple years —

sheets of it streaming across the caliche, most of it evaporating in the hundred-degree alkaline heat, forming as thunderclouds above, then, and drifting south in that form, heading out to the ocean, where it would finally end up watering the one thing that didn't need more water, the ocean.

It was theft.

People heard about the well and came out on weekends to bathe on the bare white rocks across which it gushed, and to wash their cars on Sundays — driving out onto the rocks and getting out in the ankle-deep flow and lathering their cars up with soap, then tossing buckets of that frigid, centuries-old miracle water onto the hoods and roofs and doors of their cars, washing the suds away, and then waxing and polishing their cars until they were bright gleaming dots of color, out there on the rocks, orange and yellow and green and blue and red . . .

The Catfish Man charged people fifty cents a day to come swim (or drive) in his spring. And it was his spring, for Texas still has the antiquated "rule of capture" law: however much water you can corral, from whatever source, belongs to you and no one else.

This, too, was one of the things Father was working to change in all those many long, useless meetings . . . drawing up map after map and proposing statewide water conservation plans.

Part of me wants that time back. Part of me feels robbed, as if that time were taken from me every bit as much as the water was taken from the country. But I understand too that he would not have been Father if he had not taken all those long, quixotic trips; he would have been someone else — some species more plain and brown — more common.

In time the Catfish Man stirred from his lethargy and developed his public-bathing-and-car-washing facilities into something that would gain him an agricultural exemption: a catfish farm. With investment capital from one of the county commissioners himself, he excavated huge pits in the limestone and opened up the well by drilling a thirty-inch hole into the aquifer and channeling it through limestone tanks where the swarms of catfish seethed. He fed the catfish dried cow manure and rotten corn by the dump-truck load, and in the cool water, the catfish prospered. When each tank filled in with shit and sediment, the Catfish Man would simply excavate a new pit, and divert the well's flow into that one.

Father calculated that the Catfish Man used enough water from the aquifer to meet the daily water need of 250,000 people.

Father stopped by there every time he passed. He said that there was an instant chemical dislike between the two of them — very rare for Father — but that the Catfish Man seemed to enjoy that, seemed to require an enemy, or a witness — a judge before which his actions could achieve full significance. With great glee the Catfish Man would allow Father to measure the vertical head and pressure coming out of that thirty-inch cavern, the holy river escaping. Father mapped the gradual decline of the hill country's largest artesian well for twelve years before anyone believed him. He mapped other artesian wells' declines, too, but it was this one, the Catfish Man's, where they finally, in the early 1970s, admitted that Father was right. But because of the politically untouchable "rule of capture," they claimed there was nothing they could do.

It was in that thirteenth year of Father's mapping — the year they finally believed — that even the Catfish Man's well ran dry. The Catfish Man died of a heart attack the year after that, and Father bought the four acres and welded a steel plate over that wound in the earth. He filled in the catfish pits with brush, burned the brush, and planted wildflowers. He was an old man when he did this, shaky with the loss of all that had been taken from him, and now every spring as the new county commissioners drive to work they look up the hillside at the burgeoning field of wildflowers, all the colors in nature — the field surrounded by the sprawl of trailer homes — and surely, one would think, this new generation of commissioners gets the message, that it is all hooked together, that it is all inseparable. They are, of course, too timid to act on it, but perhaps the next generation will.

*

Omar doesn't have any children, either. I suppose the land is all we will leave behind. In that way it is both our parents and our children.

The land grows flowers for me to lay at the feet of Mother's grave, there under the big tree. I cut the flowers with scissors and carry them up there, but I am just a medium, a conduit, for that flow. It is really the land that is doing it.

Unassailable. It is a gradual kind of strengthening.

*

I have not spoken enough of my younger days, my growing-up days. The first few years right after we planted her. I was in the river at least as much as I was on the land, that first year. Shuffling in the cool water, feeling crawdads and minnows scoot across the tops of my bare feet. Picking up small pebbles with my toes, lifting them up with my feet to study them in the sunlight. Stories of gold nuggets, though I never found any.

Is it odd to picnic at one's mother's grave? To sit up on the cliff and trickle pebbles over the ledge and listen to them bounce until they disappear? To eat an apple, to feel the sun, and to remember her, she who gave so much that it will never diminish? Is it odd to live with her in you, to continue to share your days and thoughts with the presence of her loving spirit?

I remember one of the last things Mother said to us, one of the very last things. In my mind, it has become the last thing, and maybe it was.

She was lying on the cedar frame bed in the back bedroom in the early summer, with the bed moved over right against the window. The window was open to let the breeze and birdsong and sunlight in, the light rushing in through the lace curtains. She had lost a lot of weight and had had a hard time, but was never more beautiful in the way that there can be nothing more beautiful than dignity.

"I've seen a lot," she said, and smiled, and it was not an act for us, it was not a thing said for our benefit. She was just saying it, and smiling. She was just brave, was all.

*

We went to the ocean once — to Padre Island, way south, down near Brownsville. We drove right out on the beach in Chubb's black Cadillac. There was no one else around. We built a fire and set up a tent. We thought we understood about tides, could see the high-water mark of the driftwood, but that was just last week's driftwood. It was a full moon, and that night while we were around the campfire, listening to the coyotes and looking up at the moon, Chubb looked out at the dark shiny vastness of the water and said, "I believe that ocean is coming closer."

Grandfather said, "Aww, *bullshit*," but the rest of us had the feeling — though we'd never been to the ocean before — that Chubb was right, and we looked at the driftwood line again. Father got up, trying to be casual about it, and sauntered down to get another piece of driftwood for the fire, but when he came back he seemed a little rushed, and he said, "That water's gotten a *lot* closer."

"Bullshit," Grandfather said, and lit a cigar: took deep, satisfied puffs, leaned his head back, and aimed his cigar-clouds at the moon. But we could hear the waves. Even Omar and I understood we weren't in river country anymore, and that the rules had changed: that in fact, there might not be any rules, down in this strange and terrible flat land.

We could *feel* the ocean — could feel the waves coming closer. It was not a good feeling to be sitting there in the dark, not knowing how much nearer the ocean was going to come, but knowing in our children's hearts — and I think Mother and Father and Chubb knew this, too — that it was certainly at least going to come over and through the spot where we were sitting.

"Pop, do you think we ought to move the car back a little?" Mother asked. "Just to be safe? It wouldn't *hurt* anything."

Even Grandfather had to admit by this point that it was an exceptionally high tide. It began to lick at the lowermost edges of the driftwood piles.

"Never show weakness before an enemy," he growled. "Stand your ground. It'll be all right."

Mother looked at him for a long moment and then stood up and began taking the tent down. If it had been Chubb or Father doing that, Grandfather would have barked them back down into submission, I think, but it was his daughter, and he said nothing.

Like zombies, the rest of us sat there in line, five monkeys on a log, and watched the white curl of foam come sweeping in under our feet, making the fire hiss and sputter, then sliding out again, carrying small pieces of our fire with it, back to the strange and ominous moonlit life source of the ocean's maw. We did not understand it, and we had the undeniable feeling that it did not care whether we did or not.

"Stand your ground," Grandfather coached us. He lit another cigar. Behind us, I could hear Mother cursing as she moved the tent and sleeping bags to higher ground. The moon was bright on the beach, had everything lit in a deep kind of whiteness, except for the total shimmering blackness of the ocean. It seemed a thousand feet deep, not a stone's throw away.

"Stand your ground," Grandfather said again, a mantra, as the water came back. I imagined that coming in with it were stingrays and jellyfish and sharks, and that they were all coming for us, tasty mountain-bait sitting like frightened rabbits in the moonlight on a log.

This time the water crashed into our fire, swept past us at ankle depth. We jumped up, yelling, as hissing pieces of the fire scattered and swirled among us, and as the ocean receded, it carried the log we'd been sitting on (a huge one) a short distance back toward its center. The retreating tide sucked the sand out from beneath our bare feet.

Grandfather looked down at his wet ankles as if the rules of physics, and his family, and the very earth itself had betrayed him. But I think even he believed that the ocean was after him, at that point — and out in the moonlight, the waves' thunder seemed to grow louder, and the waves seemed to double in size, as if emboldened by the taste of the salt-sweat from our legs.

Father was in the car, turning the spray-drenched engine over, trying to get it to start — finally it caught — and he threw it in reverse and tried to back out ahead of the next tide-sweep, but the car was stuck, the sand having been washed out from under the tires, and Chubb and Grandfather ran to the front of the car to help push it away from the hungry ocean just as the next waves hit, knee-high this time, and Omar and I were pushing, too, half pushing and half just hanging on, frightened by the waves behind us, and by the car's oily sputterings and roaring in front of us — hot sulfury steam in our faces as we leaned in against the radiator and pushed — and Mother came charging down into the backwash and helped push too. Wet sand churned straight up like a geyser, and we groaned and cursed and pushed like, I suppose, giving birth — our cheeks turned sideways and our teeth gritted and neck muscles strained

tight as cables — and finally, as the next waves came in behind us, we got the car moving with the force of fear as
much as strength, and as if wrestling some great anguished
draft horse out of the mud, we got the car going, got it up
into the dunes, but still Father kept driving. He kept the car
in reverse and backed another three hundred yards into the
dunes.

We gathered our sleeping bags and gear and followed
him, like nomads, out into the brush. We walked in a pro-
cession, dragging our sleeping bags, the moon shining
bright on our backs. Grandfather came last. We lay our
sleeping bags out willy-nilly, as if having fallen from the
stars, and didn't even bother setting up the tent. From a distance, the surf sounded gently reassuring, but still our
hearts pounded in wet ocean-fear, and our legs tingled from
where the ocean had caressed and then seized them, and the
last thing Chubb said before we all fell asleep was, "Hey
Frank, do you want me to sleep up on the top of the car
tonight and keep a lookout?"

*

In the morning we awoke to a pink sunrise. We fixed
breakfast and then went down to the beach. The ocean
seemed very far away, and was almost flat. It almost seemed
like our friend again. We wore straw hats and walked on
the beach all day, picking up shells. I wanted to see flamin-
gos, but Father and Grandfather cursed bitterly and said
they'd almost all been killed so that their feathers could be
put in women's hats, which made me feel somewhat bad in
general for being a girl — a kind of strange, hurt hopeless-
ness — *it wasn't me!* — but then Father put his hand on
my back and reminded Grandfather that it had been men
doing the killing, and Grandfather looked off at the ocean
in the direction of Florida, and seemed embarrassed, even
ashamed. Mother and Omar caught up with us and we
walked together until we came to a tidal inlet where gulls

and terns were splashing in the shallows, feeding on crabs and small fish. Their wings were filled with light, and we sat and watched for an hour, the six of us. A flock of thirty sandhill cranes flew over us, as big as bombers, wings flapping slowly, necks and legs outstretched, flying as if they were swimming through the sky, and a few of them uttered their great sonorous croaks as they spotted us below. Mother reached out and took my hand and squeezed it.

I'd hate to have to choose what the single most beautiful thing I've seen is.

*

We napped in our tent, sweetly feverish, mildly delirious. In the winter-short evening we cooked venison steaks on another driftwood fire, watching the ocean somewhat warily. Omar and I flew a kite after supper until dark while the grown-ups watched. There was a warm southwest wind blowing right before dark and I know what I did then was evil and trashy, but it was just a balsa-wood-and-paper kite. I took it from Omar's hands and released it — he started to cry — but when he heard the grown-ups sitting on the log cheer the kite as it went far out to sea, he stopped crying and began to laugh.

That night we stepped in the calm sea with kerosene lanterns and gigs, looking for flounder, all six of us strung out and wading with the lanterns whose light floated just above the water. We moved slowly, each of us away from all the others, searching intently, and from the beach it must have looked as if we were fireflies. Grandfather had cautioned us repeatedly about not mistaking, under the lantern's glow, the shadow of our own foot for a flounder.

Omar got the first one; he held it up, thrashing on the end of his gig, and whooped. Mother got the second one. The flounders must have known something was up, after that, because for a long time we didn't see any, but it didn't matter: we saw all kinds of little ghost crabs and minnows and mullet and skates passing beneath the light of our lanterns, little creatures going in and out with the tide, and best of all were the schools of shrimp, whose eyes glowed fiery red in the lights from our lanterns — devil shrimp! — and whose bodies absorbed that bright light. Glowing as they leapt through the waves, the shrimp were as luminous as ghosts, as they took our lantern light with them.

Father caught a flounder, finally, and Chubb caught a big one, and that was enough for breakfast. Father called for us all to head in, and we waded back to shore, our lights converging as one.

We stayed on the beach for four days. I think it was in February. Sometimes in the day we'd go off into the Laguna Madre, just exploring — a vast salt flat, perfectly horizontal, dotted with a few saltbush and creosote plants. We'd see a jackrabbit with his great ears sticking up, not forty yards away, and in the heat-shimmer and salt haze we couldn't get a fix on perspective — there was nothing around that was taller than us, and not a shadow anywhere — and we'd become convinced in that shimmer that we were seeing a large deer, a buck with antlers, about five hundred yards away. We'd set out after the deer, wondering why a deer would have antlers in winter, and we would be almost upon the rabbit before he came to his senses and bolted into zig-zag flight, coming so suddenly into focus — *rabbit* — that our bodies, our minds, were deceived further, and it seemed for a moment not as if it had been a mistake on our part, but as if there had been a magic trick: as if the earth itself, that strange salt country, had changed a deer into a rabbit in the blink of an eye.

At the end I was glad to be heading home, riding in the back seat with the window down, feeling cool air turn colder as we headed back north. I knew Chubb would be relieved to get back home to the light in his cabin, and though we'd had a wonderful time, there was a sweet and unmistakable feeling, with each mile that passed, that we were leaving a somewhat ominous and threatening place, and going back to a place of immense safety and security, peace and comfort. I sat in the back with Omar napping against my right shoulder and Mother napping against my left, and I thumbed through the bird book and looked at pictures of all the new birds I had seen, and at the ones I had not seen. It was unimaginable to think that they were out there — all these hundreds, even thousands of birds — and that I had not seen them. I felt both hungry and sated — like a cat, I imagined. With Mother asleep on my shoulder, good crisp air coming in the window, a stomach full of flounder, and two dozen new birds flying through my mind — and returning *home* — I felt like there couldn't be a more satisfied person in the world.

This, in turn, made me hungrier: made me want to see more.

We got back around five in the evening, just before dark, sun-browned and road weary, but I was out of the car and running even before Father had the trunk open to unpack. I ran past the swimming hole, past the little dam to the river — dusk was coming down fast now, floating in from out of the bare-limbed trees — a pair of wood ducks jumped up from the river and flew downstream, making their high strange squeal — and I made my way across the river and up onto the mountain, and into the junipers, scrambling, as the moon came up over the trees. I had to make sure it was all still there. I picked up rocks, squeezing them; bit the ends of juniper needles and tasted their turpentine sap. I went up to the cliff and sat and felt my heart thumping inside. I breathed the cold air and watched the moon climb higher until it, and all of the country below, was mine again.

*

In the early sixties, I went to school with a girl whose father was president of a ranchers' social organization known as the Predator Club. Their headquarters was out west, on the county line, in a leaning shack with dusty windows and one bare light bulb overhead. It was next to the bar (the Starlight), and as county agent, Father would sometimes stop by the Predator Club's meetings, mostly to just let them know he was alive and in the world. They didn't like him and he didn't like them. Complicating Father's duties and life was the fact that in theory part of his job description was to act as a liaison for those ranchers seeking governmental assistance (poison, aerial machine gunning, and so on) in eradicating predators (foxes, coyotes, bobcats, crows, owls, raccoons, jackrabbits, mountain lions — the whole food chain) from their ranch lands. Father always refused to help them, though, saying it was against his religious beliefs.

These men saw Prade Ranch as a breeding ground for the wild beasts who would then come in the night and make raids on their brain-dead cattle herds and their range-maggot stinking sprawls of sheep.

The ranchers received free poison, and received bounties for the predators they killed. It was all a huge game, like chopping firewood for the winter: seeing who could gather the biggest stack of dead wild animals to take in for bounties. At the Predator Club meetings, the men would drink, shoot pool, play cards, tell stories, and strengthen their social bonds, while out on the prairie, to the north and east, the full moon rose, the wild creatures came carefully out of their burrows, stirred in their nests: fed their young, and listened to the far-off sound of a truck out on a country road, or the sound of some ranch dog barking . . . They waited for the sounds of man to cease, around two or three in the morning, so that they could then come out and have three or four hours before daylight, when the world that was once theirs would be returned to them, late in this century of loss, and of fear . . .

Although federal law prohibited the killing of endangered species such as golden and bald eagles, state law did not, and the feds were a long way away. There wasn't anything Father could do to get the Predator Club to stop killing coyotes and crows, but he let them know if he caught them killing eagles, he would do his best to send them to jail.

I know that they would have killed him, to keep from going to jail.

During that time of the Predator Club — those monthly meetings — happiness left our home, and we'd be tense, even irritable. Sometimes (unknown to my father), Chubb and Grandfather would ride out with guns and park in the dark and keep hidden watch on the Predator Club meetings that my father attended.

We all knew they shot at eagles, chased them in helicopters. They didn't dare fly over Prade Ranch — several years earlier, Grandfather had fired his rifle at the helicopter and put a hole in the rear fuselage. He could very easily have hit the gas tank ("I was aiming for the gas tank," he told us, but in court he had to say that he was just firing a warning shot, and that he hadn't meant to hit them . . .).

But still, especially in the spring, we'd hear the helicopters, hear the gunfire. The eagles congregated in larger and larger numbers above our canyon, drifting on the thermals. I believe without a moment's hesitation they gave us a blessing, that the accumulated weight of their bronze-gold wingbeats made it a holy spot, both for them and for us.

I heard Mother and Father whispering about it some nights; I heard Grandfather and Father talking about it, always growing quiet whenever I came in the room — they who had never been quiet around me, so that I knew it was a dangerous thing.

The girl I went to school with — the daughter of a sheep rancher, the Predator Club's president — there was something wrong with her — something missing — some ability to take joy from life, some *mercy.* The rest of us shied away from her because of this strange sickness that emanated from her. It wasn't her fault, but still, like healthy animals shunning a sick one, we avoided her, even all the ranchers' sons and daughters whose fathers were in the Predator Club with her — Alicia's — father.

She just wasn't right.

Being cast out, of course, aggravated her condition — her otherness — and because in many respects I had my own otherness, my own certain distance from the herd, Alicia turned her resentment on me. She watched me. Even in her eyes, she was not right. Sometimes I'd feel that there was so much sickness in her that it was spilling out of her, and that wherever she looked, that sickness would spread.

I am trying to remember all the pleasant things about the country — all the good things — but there was this, too, and like the good things, it also was, I suppose, part of the gradual strengthening, part of the process whereby one becomes wedded to the land, becomes laid down into it, heart and memory and soul, like a formation of rock: a *family*. A generation, or two or three.

What I mean to say is that I have two things, two secrets, that I am not proud of, growing up. These things are part of the land, too, now, and part of me.

The first thing was the golden eagle I found along the river one September. At first I thought it was a man wearing feathers, it was so large. The day was extraordinarily still — everything seemed frozen, with only the river moving past — and I thought that the eagle, or man, was only sleeping, and so I approached carefully, tiptoeing over the white-bleached rocky shoals: certain that my approach would cause the man, or the eagle, to wake up and fly away.

The closer I got, the more luminous the body seemed to get, the bronze feathers becoming even more bronze in that late September sunlight, and I could see that there were injuries — broken feet, a fractured wing, and several bullet holes across the wide, feathered back — but still I believed that the man, or eagle, was only resting, and that it would get up and fly away.

Even when I sat down next to it and touched it, I believed that it was only resting.

I sat next to the bloody rocks (in my tears it seemed that the white caliche, the soil itself, was bleeding — that the blood had not come from the eagle, but up from the ground itself) and I rested my hand on the eagle's back, whose feathers were warm in the sun, and whose eyes were closed (beautiful blue eyelids, like a man's). But when the sun went down behind the ridge the body began to grow cool, then cold, and I lay down and covered as much of it as I could with my body, to keep it warm.

Later, long after nightfall, I woke up and heard the bell ringing, and left my shirt over the eagle's back and hurried home.

I did not tell my father, or anyone, about the eagle. I didn't want our lives to change. I didn't want to bear testimony.

The next morning when I went back out at dawn — running, to rejoin the eagle — I stopped when I saw that my shirt was off the eagle, and I thought that the eagle had gotten up and moved around in the night, trying to heal itself. But when I got to the eagle I saw that it was deader than the day before, and that the wind must have just blown the shirt off.

I spent that day and the next (a Sunday) carrying the eagle across the river and up to the cliffs. It was much taller than I was, and heavier. I kept falling and cutting myself. I'd stop and rest and feel how the talons were like swords. I'd open one of the eagle's eyes and stare into it. I'd stroke the great curved beak.

By Saturday night when Mother rang the bell for me to come in, I had the eagle almost to the top of the mountain

— I shed my clothes at the river and bathed before dressing again and hurrying home — and then on Sunday, I got the eagle to the top of the mountain.

I carried it to the deepest, thickest woods I knew of, up above the cliffs — the river so far below it was like only a thread — and I climbed up in a big dead oak that hung out over the canyon and placed the eagle's body in a fork of the dead oak. The oak was dry and hollow-rotty, and pieces of it cracked and crumbled and spilled over the edge of the cliff, vaporized into dust-nothings as they fell to the river so far below that they would never reach it — and with leather strips I lashed the eagle high in the tree, in this place where the river could be seen below but where the eagle could not be seen (backdrop of tall cedar obscuring the skyline: the eagle *hiding*), and I bound the eagle's wings so that they were outspread, seven feet wide, uplifted as if on a crucifix, and I tied his head upright so that he could see all below, and all beyond, and lashed his feet to the branch, curled those steel talons into and around the wood so they would never let go. The wind was always blowing up on the ridgeline, and it blew and ruffled his feathers, and when I left, he was still sitting like that, head up and wings out-stretched, ready at any moment, in any life, to take flight: poised at the edge, *ready.*

That night I dreamed of the oak tree flying; that the eagle had taken flight and carried the great tree away with him, the tree bound to his ankles. It was a windy night, gusting and straining against our tin roof, and I got up and went outside to look at the moon and to watch the sky, to see if I would see the great bird carrying the giant tree away, but I saw nothing, only clouds and moon, yet there was a kind of an echo, as if I had just missed it: as if, had I come out on the porch a second earlier, I would have seen it.

I was sick for a week after that, in bed with a high fever, and when I next went back to check on the eagle, the feathers were beginning to come off. I took one off and carried it home to keep in my cedar chest, where it still rests — but the eagle's grip on that branch remained as firm as ever, until by the time I went away to college there was only the skeleton of the eagle, wind whistling through the bones, through the eye sockets, making a whistling sound perhaps not unlike the sound eagles make to themselves as they fly two miles above the earth — this eagle skeleton holding up the tree's skeleton — and then one year when I came home from college, the tree and the eagle were gone. I crawled to the edge of the cliff and looked down, but saw nothing.

*

The second thing I am not proud of is also a sin of omission. The girl I went to school with, the one whose scent was different — the one no one liked, without knowing why — the girl whose father was president of the Predator Club — told us what her father did with lambs.

She was bragging, trying for friends, or even for a touch, a whisper of intimacy. The Predator Club kept a running list in the newspaper of the number of livestock suspected of having been killed by predators. (If a lamb disappeared, or was found dead — even if uneaten, or unscavenged — it was also counted as killed-by-predators.) One of the duties of the members of the Predator Club involved a conscious effort to keep predators under sustained negative light. The members wrote regular letters-to-the-editor detailing the stock they'd lost, and to which predator, and in which grisly manner. (I was reminded of the game that Omar and I played as children: seizing a turkey drumstick and shaking it back and forth, pretending that it was a human arm or leg.)

Each issue of the weekly paper had at least one letter that detailed graphically the wild savagery seething out in the brush, just out of sight — the evil that pulsed beneath the fur of the wild things. A visitor to Real County would think the human race was under attack.

> It is spring again and I have lost another babe lamb to the wolf of the sky, the feathered Adolf Hitler — the gold eagle come out of the sun and struck lamb and ewe and pulled there [sic] entrils out and flew away with entrils hanging like a joke, smiling . . .

and

> I have seen mother coyotes teach their young how to torment, tossing mice in the air repeatedly, torturing them. These kinds of coyotes are a danger to humans and also have lots of diseases. They chase pregnant mama cows on moonlit nights until the fetus is aborted and then do a victory dance around the stillborn calf, yaping [sic] and dancing but never touching the carcass . . .

and often, a variation (or sometimes direct reprint) of this one:

> My grandfather came here in ought-eight and fought hard to get rid of all the varmints. That poison the land with their evil. I don't know why his work should go for not. He made sure the Indians didn't come back too so it is safe for God-fearing hard-working white people! People are more important than skunks, and so all skunks and other predators should be killed. Skunks eat turkey eggs! Did you know that?

In the spring when I was fourteen — imagining, through myself, what she had been like when she was fourteen — there was a rash of eagle predation on the great herds of sheep that scoured the hillsides of Real County. The state officials (who were owned by the agriculture industry) condoned the eagle killings that followed; the feds did not, and they sent some of their men in to break it up. One of those federal men was shot and wounded. There were rumors that my father was not a county employee, but a fed also: an informer. The only thing that saved him perhaps was his outspokenness against eagle-killing; if he'd been an informer, he would've been quiet and secretive, like a fox.

He was like a crow or an owl, however: scolding, calling out. Every spring we'd see between ten and twenty golden eagles, including some nesting pairs. (They mate for life.) That year — the year that Mother's life in the rocks was in its second year — that year, we saw only one golden eagle. We didn't find any poisoned animals on Prade Ranch, but Father said he was finding them on the roadsides, in his travels: 1080, he suspected.

He said that neighbors were acting differently, whenever he stopped in.

Father picked up some of the robins and rabbits and raccoons and dogs and cats and foxes and squirrels he found on the roadside and sent them all to Austin to be tested.

1080 and massive doses of strychnine.

The land was aching with poison. For the first time, we were afraid to drink the water straight from the river, as we'd done all our lives.

Outside of our ranch, the world seemed to consist of nothing but sheep, cows, and goats. Sheep, cows, goats. The mohair market was up that year, and goats especially flooded the hills. Whenever I got off of Prade Ranch it was like a foreign country.

The girl at school who bragged, Alicia, told us things about her father. About the eagle claws he kept: about the necklace he'd made her of their beaks and talons, and how she kept it buried in a cedar box, in a secret place.

No one believed her. But as eagle killings continued to

be in the news, she kept insisting that her father had killed hundreds, and that she had all their talons, that they were strung on leather, made into bracelets and necklaces, and that they kept them hidden "because of the g.d. feds."

All right, so where are they hidden? we wanted to know. *Prove it.* But Alicia only shook her head, said that she couldn't. She said her father had said the whole family would go to jail forever if the g.d. feds found out.

Bull, we said. *Liar.* And turned away, annoyed that we'd paused to listen to the clatter of her tinny words but delighted by the delicious taste of blood, delighted by the anguish we could feel descending upon her as we drifted away. It was like — we knew this in our minds, could taste it — like pulling a sheet back and walking away with it, leaving her bare body exposed, a quivering body that's been burned badly and needs that sheet's cool light touch to give the body a moment's peace, even a moment's ecstasy . . .

Bull, we said, pulling that sheet back as we walked away. The other girls would wander off to play and I would wander off to stand under a tree and read . . .

She was quiet about it then for a long time. My guess is that someone at school mentioned it to his or her father, who was in the club, who then mentioned it to Alicia's father, who doubtless roared at Alicia.

But in May, too lonely to stand it, she began mentioning it again. *Bull,* everyone said, but this time I saw it was for real. This time I could feel what I had missed before. And she must have seen the way I looked at her and believed, then — the way I did not say *bull* when all the other boys and girls did.

I turned away and went over to my tree to read. But this time it did not feel like we were pulling the blanket away because this time someone — me — had left her with hope.

Three days later she came over to my tree at recess and pulled one of the eagle-bracelets out of a brown paper bag, and just held it there, until I reached out and touched it, pressed my fingers against the points of the talons, to see that it was real.

I looked at her and saw her for the first time.

She was so blind in her fear — like a girl put in a closet and shouted at, and kept in that closet, not let out until after dark — that she couldn't even think, or consider, who my father was. She was so desperate that it didn't matter; there was only the moment. I touched the razor talons, almost pierced the tip of my finger against them, and I believed: I believed then and still do that that moment may have saved her, may have pulled her out of the ocean in which she was drowning, sinking like an anvil . . .

We never became friends. We never even talked again. But I'd look at her in class sometimes, and she'd see me, and she'd know then that she existed — that even if she wasn't loved, or popular, neither was she invisible — that had ended the moment I'd touched the eagle's talons — and I marveled at how much power and magic animals have, and what the eagle had, even after death.

We have traded away our mysticism for a few ears of corn, for a crop of maize, or chickens, or cows, or trinkets.

I did not tell my father. And when I heard Alicia bragging later in the spring that her father killed eagles by staking a lamb out as a lure — sometimes waiting for as long as three days before an eagle came down on the sickly, strange-acting lamb — I did not tell my father that, either.

By the school year's end, Alicia was showing other classmates a bracelet one day, a necklace the next. I never saw her get anywhere that same punch of awareness from any of them that she got from me that one time, though I would see her chasing it until finally she gave up and returned to her solitary outpost.

The Predator Club no longer exists. I would like to say that it is because all of its members grew older and more feeble — and that much is true — but it was gone long before that, gone shortly after I went off to college, gone because there were no more predators to kill. Rabbits moved in and overgrazed the last blades and shallow roots of grass that the cows and sheep didn't get. Without coyotes, hawks, and eagles to cull the rabbits, the pastures disappeared, blew away to Mexico. By the time I went off to school, only the Prade Ranch had a few predators remaining, holed up in the woods I had so safely and lovingly crawled through as a girl, both with and without Omar. The rabbits cycle low to high every seven years, but without predators, the highs are higher than ever, obscenely so.

The year I went off to school was at the high of a seven-year cycle, and when I'd drive home on weekends (I went to San Marcos my first year), there were so many rabbits on the roads at night that it was impossible to miss them. They ran out suddenly in front of the headlights and then stopped. I'd swerve the truck to miss one and would hit another one. It was like driving down a road littered with breadfruit: thump thump, thump thump, thump thump. It was impossible to miss them, and it made me angry.

In the daytime you'd see them limping down the roads and out in the dust-pastures with great lumps on their backs and sides where tapeworm larvae had developed under the skin. I remember there were more flies around the county that year than anyone could ever remember seeing. Every rabbit carcass seethed with maggots. I watched the sky for eagles, for hawks, but there were none, just dry blue heat.

Did I assist in the slaughter of those eagles, by not telling my father? Could he have stopped it — could he have saved them? Even now my cheeks burn to realize that, with the knowledge, maybe he could have.

Maybe he would've gotten killed too, though, and he was and is my own eagle, the last one. I don't know. I know that even by the time I was eighteen, I believed I should have shared with him what I knew.

So when I hit all those rabbits, driving up and down the back roads — when I felt all those sick, soft thuds under the wheels of the truck — I set my jaw, and didn't slow down, and I took my medicine: I kept going, streaking through their midst at sixty miles an hour, like some terrible angel of death streaking down from the sky. All those extra diseased rabbits were mine, and I knew what I had to do. Every *thump* under the tires felt as if it were me who'd been struck, not the rabbit. I was both predator and prey: I was everything. Every *atom* of me was Real County.

*

We cooked out down by the river my first weekend home from college. It was all new, and we didn't yet have a ceremony for it, a tradition, so we kept on with the old one and waited for a new one to develop.

We did what we had always done. We sat on the oak benches in the old vine-covered limestone gazebo and looked at the deep still pool of water, where our long-ago family had dammed a little bend of the Nueces below Chubb's cabin (whose light was still burning, now in his eighty-seventh year).

Father cooked a venison ham over the low coals of the barbecue grill, spooning a *putanesco* sauce over the meat again and again, and splashing river water on the coals to make the mesquite smoke rise. It was early October, and the dry leaves still clung to the yellow hickories, ash, and oaks. They rattled in the breeze. The pecan trees were already bare, their leaves and leftover nutmeat rotting back into the black thin soil and helping give the river its river smell.

The garlic and butter smells of the nutmeat deepened as dusk fell, and so did the odor of the sweet potatoes baking in the coals. I sat next to Omar on the bench facing the river with my arm around him and looked at the cliff wall right in front of us — the one we never dived off of. The mother raven's nest was still there, left over from the spring, built in a cliff recess with heavy branches and the thigh bones of cattle. The bones in the nest shone bright in the subdued light. I felt Mother coming up the river to join us, and I tightened my arm around Omar. I tried to remember what it had been like when I was twelve.

Father was handsome: still straight-backed, strong-shouldered. Still lean. His hair was gray, on its way to becoming as silver as Chubb's and Grandfather's. I looked at the two older men who were sitting together on the lower bench, the one closest to the river, watching the dimness come in through the trees. They were both wearing sweaters, though the night did not strike me as being cold. They were sitting there not saying anything, their shoulders hunched and hands wrapped around clay cups of steaming coffee, watching Mother drift upriver to join us, still young and beautiful.

With each passing year Chubb was becoming bolder, stronger, venturing farther and farther into dusk, to stay with Grandfather longer, before hurrying back to his stone house and its familiar, all-night yellow lantern light. Even now I saw him turn and study the red sky in the west, his old eyes gauging the minutes; then he turned his head back to the river and said something to Grandfather, who grunted. Grandfather got up, leaning on the cane he used now (a deer antler for a handle), and creaked over to the gazebo and flicked on the light switch, sending a beam of high-intensity light onto the cliff wall, and the trees around us, and the river, the pool, below us.

For Chubb, we would do this — would wash out the stars. We would push back the lovely night.

Omar and I blinked in the bright light. Father kept cooking. Grandfather hobbled over and, leaning on his cane, touched my face with the back of his crooked old hand; held it there, smiling, then did the same to Omar. Then he went back down to sit with Chubb again.

Look, Omar, I wanted to say, *look: they're old men. Not even ten years ago, they were younger, were digging postholes and riding horses through the woods and walking across the hills, the mountains, and now . . . look.*

Later in the night, as we ate the deer and drank the red wine, the screech owls began to shriek, just before going out hunting. An elf owl flew right over the pool, even under all that bright light — there was no mistaking it for an elf — and Grandfather and I jumped up, so excited we spilled our plates of food, for we'd never seen an elf owl out here, not in all our years. They weren't supposed to be found this far east.

"Arra-oh!" Grandfather cried, pointing. *"Elf owl!"*

We waited and watched, daring to hope that the owl would return, would fly past once more, but it didn't. We finally sat down, still exuberant, and looked at each other, grinning. It was as if we had seen Mother herself. A bold raccoon came from out of the darkness and began eating the meat Grandfather and I had spilled when we jumped up. I fixed Grandfather and myself a new plate. The big raccoon just stayed there, in the middle of our circle, eyes bright in the light, watching us watch it back, chewing on the meat it held in its delicate hands, smacking its lips and then licking its beautiful long whiskers and standing up on its hind legs, looking around for more.

*

Chubb died later that fall. I was rooming with a girl from Amarillo when Father called me in my dorm room, the first and only time he was ever to call, while I was in college; he dreaded and despised telephones.

"Chubb's dead," was the first thing he said. "He just didn't wake up this morning."

"Are you sure?" I asked — the dumbest question of my

life. That terrible drowning feeling — of no longer being able to get a thing you need — *air*. It felt like I was eight again. *Chubb's not dead, he's just sleeping.*

"Can you come home?" my father asked. His voice seemed smaller — different somehow — and he was a different man, like a snake or insect that sheds its skin, or the caterpillar that becomes a moth.

My father had not gone to college. He was asking if I could come home as if college were some kind of prison.

*

I drove with the windows down. It was the first week in November, and deer season had not yet started. The light was shimmery. I was the only one out on the road. I left San Marcos by way of the Devil's Backbone, got up on its spine and looked out at all the blue juniper country, all the deep dark pockets and folds that were my heartland: that was me, had become me. I listened to the old tires of my truck hum *smack smack smack* against the worn highway. Vultures floated on the thermals rising out of the canyons. The sun was out, but it was a cool day. I thought about not going back to school. I knew only one place, one ten-thousand-acre piece of land. What about Africa, Costa Rica, Alaska, and Russia? What about Canada, Hawaii, and Tibet? What about Romania, Bolivia, and New Zealand?

Farther west, a raven floated down the road like an escort, a companion, making sure I got home all right.

*

Omar was still in junior high school. Father and Grandfather were sitting in the den, sitting in the rawhide chairs, heads down, remembering. I imagined they had been listening for me, but still had not heard me drive up, which made me realize how old they really were: Grandfather, old beyond his time, and Father, old before his time. Two old men, looking defeated. It made me angry.

They rose when I came in the den, and we hugged, and then they wanted to sit back down and act all lost and bereaved, but I couldn't stand to see them like that, so I made them get in the truck and go with me to find a burial spot.

"Have you told his family?" I asked, and Grandfather shook his head and mumbled some grief sound that even I, with a knowledge of his stroke language, couldn't interpret.

"He says they're almost all dead, too," Father said. "No phone in the village. They're almost all gone, anyway. A few great-nieces and -nephews. A younger brother and sister, I think. I'm not sure."

Grandfather made another sound of mourning. I didn't understand it as words at first, and I left the road and drove down into the river, looking for the old Uvalde road, and the wagon ruts. The water was low, and we drove down the center of the river for a while, with the bright white cliffs reflecting on either side of us. The peeling bark of sycamores. I pointed to a red-tailed hawk half a mile above us. I watched the hawk to see if it was Chubb. Strange things happen in the animal world when a loved one dies, that's a fact. They honor our passage with far more reverence than we do theirs.

Grandfather was still making his sounds, and I realized he was trying to talk. I stopped the truck and turned it off so I could hear better. The river continued to riffle past us, a sad, cleansing sound.

He took out his pen and notepad.

"We talked about it," he wrote. "He wanted to be burned, like me. He was a Catholic but he said whatever I wanted is what he wanted."

Burned. I had no idea how to do it. I was used to planting — but to burn — I found myself thinking of crops.

Grandfather was scribbling in his notepad again. "Up on a scaffolding," he wrote. "Like the Indians. You do it with cedar. Cedar burns real hot."

"Did he know he was going to die?" I asked, and Grandfather looked at me in surprise — his little granddaughter
again.

"He was eighty-seven," he said in his stroke language.
Grandfather studied my face carefully then, missing nothing. He watched my face the way he would have watched
the cedars for a songbird he was trying to lure in with his
screech owl calls. I was the young woman who would be
burying him. He was trying to have it both — the afterlife
and the here. His face was as curious as a young boy's.

"He knew that he was going to die *sometime,*" he said in
his groaning, hesitant syllables . . . the speech that was so
unlike the flights of birds.

*

We built a scaffolding out of dead cedar. We built it ten feet
high, on the banks of the river where we'd decided to set
him. Omar and Father helped, while Grandfather super-
vised. It was good for Omar to see this, good for him to
help. He was thirteen, and in some ways on his own for the
first time.

I think even then I knew Omar would be going away,
would be leaving the land to explore cities and towns. But
still I tried as hard as I could — *it was my job* — to plant a
sense of the wild within him: something that calls one back
into the interior, back into the shadows and safety of a
place that still has reverence to it. Within every atom of it.

*

We built the fire hot: piled cedar beneath the scaffolding all
the way up to and over the top of the scaffolding. He had-
n't been looking so good, and in the daytime one of us had
always had to sit around and stand guard to keep the vultures and eagles and ravens off of him (when it was my
turn, I'd sometimes let them land on him and take a peck or

two, but then I'd shoo them away. I'd watch them fly away downriver, rising into the sun with a sun-hot piece of Chubb in their bellies).

At night, we kept kerosene lanterns burning around him.

The body knows, as does the spirit. The leftover, cooling electricity of the body winding down; the increasing dynamo-hum of the spirit being truly born . . .

Ceremony. When we've lost that, we've lost everything, and are only wandering in the dark, like chickens or lambs waiting for eagles.

We must participate in this world that has birthed us. We must not sit around in rawhide rocking chairs with our heads sunk in grief, while the waters trickle past. We must join the waters.

*

We burned him on a Saturday, burned him good, and felt his spirit rise with the smoke. While the fire was raging, we saw a small brown creature swimming upstream. I thought at first it was an otter or a beaver, but then realized it was a nutria, an animal like a muskrat that had been introduced to the Louisiana marshes in the thirties, and had since worked its way over to the Gulf Coast.

This nutria must have worked its way up the river systems — the Guadalupe, the Pedernales, the Frio, Medina, and Nueces — traveling by some strange urge to keep swimming to where the water was clear, not muddy. It had to be the first nutria to ever hit Real County, and as the fire raged, the nutria kept motoring upstream, and I felt better about burning Chubb up here in the mountains, instead of down in Mexico. *We belong with our parents,* I thought, but the nutria kept going, and Chubb belonged with Grandfather, with us . . .

*

Which ashes were his, and which were those of the cedar? Grandfather said that Chubb's ashes would be more blue, would almost glow in the dark, due to the phosphorus in them, while the cedar ashes would be mostly white. We walked through the coals and ashes that night with metal buckets and little garden shovels, searching for those that glowed in the dark. Some of the larger cedar stumps still glowed red-hot: we wore our heavy hiking boots. Grandfather waded in the hot ashes leaning on his cane, with Father holding him by one arm, and Omar searched for the blue ashes too, sometimes shining a little flashlight at something, so that I was reminded of when we had gone searching for flounders, out in the waves so long ago.

We put the blue ashes in an old can Chubb had always used to water his garden with. We washed and waxed his beloved '49 Cadillac, and though the tires were rotted off, we managed to pull the car down to the river, and pushed it right up against the cliff, up on shore, under a mossy overhang. We put the top down, set the urn in the front seat.

We stood there barefooted, ankle-deep in the cold clear water, when it was all done. Deer season had opened that weekend, and all morning we'd heard the sounds of that strange war. A kind of trespassing, where too often people hunted and killed a thing that was not a part of them, nor were they a part of it.

We'd honored the end of his life, but as we stood there, his death seemed incomplete, unfinished, without Mother there to grieve for him. We just stood around as if not quite knowing what to do. I realized that even though I was eighteen and not yet as strong as I one day hoped to become, I had to step up and take charge. Everyone else was too young or too old or too male. I had to finish up Chubb, and had to finish the ceremony, much as she would have. She would have said something tender, I imagine, something from the grace of her heart, some assemblage of words.

I had none. I stood there with my hand on Omar's shoulder, and I made the daytime feathery sound of the screech owl — all songbirds' mortal enemy.

One by one, they began to scold — began filtering in from out of the woods, and surrounding us, flying all about, looking for the owl.

Vireos, jays, buntings, warblers — the small bright birds of life fluttered all around us, scolding, as if angry that we were letting the river drift past.

Across the river, atop that highest bluff, beneath that largest oak, I could feel Mother, young and strong and alive. I could feel the mild sunlight striking her as it shone on the side of the white limestone cliffs. I could feel the breeze moving through her.

Now we were down to four of us.

*

It was after Chubb's death that Grandfather learned to sing. I came home almost every weekend, helped him into the truck, and took him out into the brush, where he'd sit under an umbrella to protect himself from the direct sun. He'd sip tea from a mayonnaise jar and cup his hands to his mouth and make his daytime screech owl call. As he got older, his call got more wavery, more authentic: he drew in more and more birds with it.

His beautiful metallic silver hair had turned snow white over the course of just a few days following Chubb's death, and in a way this made him seem younger: made him seem to fit the white caliche landscape even better, and blend in.

His skin was turning whiter, too, even after he had been out in the sun.

It was beautiful, watching him get old — *ancient* — now that I had realized he too was going to die. This time I could understand it. It was like watching some graceful diver plunge in slow motion — the slowest — from the top of an improbably high cliff, down to the cool river below.

The way he learned to sing was by imitating the songbirds: their warbles and whistles, their scolds. Before his
stroke he'd been able to imitate certain notes and melodies
of their calls, but never whole *songs.*

I was sitting under the umbrella with him, in early
March — March second, the day the Texas Declaration of
Independence had been signed, when Grandfather began to
sing. A black-and-white warbler had flown in right in front
of us and was sitting on a cedar limb, singing — relieved,
I think, that we weren't owls. Cedar waxwings moved
through the brush behind it, pausing to wipe the bug juice
from their bills by rubbing their beaks against branches
(like men dabbing their mouths with napkins after getting
up from the table). Towhees were hopping all around us,
scratching through the cedar duff for pill bugs, pecking,
pecking, pecking, and still the vireo stayed right there on
that branch, turning its head sideways at us and singing,
and Grandfather made one deep sound in his throat — like
a stone being rolled away — and then he began to sing
back to the bird, not just imitating the warbler's call, but
singing a whole warbler song, making up warbler sentences, warbler declarations.

Other warblers came in from out of the brush and surrounded us, and still Grandfather kept whistling and trill-
ing. More birds flew in. Grandfather sang to them, too.
With high little sounds in his throat, he called in the
mourning doves and the little Inca doves that were starting
to move into this country, from the south, and whose call I
liked very much, a slightly younger, faster call that seemed
to complement the eternity-becking coo of the mourning
dove.

Grandfather sang until dark, until the birds stopped an-
swering his songs and instead went back into the brush to
go to roost, and the fireflies began to drift out of the bushes
like sparks and the coyotes began to howl and yip. Grandfather had long ago finished all the tea, sipping it between

birdsongs to keep his voice fresh, and now he was tired, too tired to even fold the umbrella. As I helped him walk back to the truck, he held the umbrella aloft, as if to keep the stars off of him. Fireflies surrounded us. Grandfather held his deer-antler cane in one hand and the umbrella in the other. I gripped his elbow and helped steady him over the loose rocks. I tried to imagine myself needing assistance over these ridges, across this hardscrabble, this heart's hard country, but couldn't.

I helped Grandfather up into the truck. Although he was as lean as ever — "still a flatbelly," I'd say, every time I came home, patting him there — he nonetheless seemed to be getting heavier, *denser,* with time, unlike so many other old men and women. It was as if he were leaden, and I wondered how he could even lift his feet.

I imagined all the minerals from all the river water he'd drunk in his life crystallizing in his veins and arteries. Glittering silicates and coppers and golds, all the rare gems and heavy minerals of the land returning to his body, claiming his body — clamoring for it, as he approached his ninetieth year away from the soil — too long! too long! — and I pictured the cool blue phosphorescence of his bones surrounding those slowly crystallizing veins, until I imagined (driving home in the dark that night) that if he were to open his mouth wide I might catch a glimpse of a diamond glittering in the moonlight behind his teeth.

Bullbats leapt and whirled before us, chasing the moths drawn to our headlights as we drove slowly home. It seemed that the bullbats were flying right at us, trying to summon us — to enlist us in their world of the night. I missed Chubb as I would miss any other part of the world in which I'd grown up in — as if the world's rules had changed, and we would no longer get our light or heat from the sun, or as if there would no longer be such a thing as rivers.

We drove up toward the house, going slowly past his

stone cabin. We had left the light burning inside, and already the trumpet vine (to which the hummingbirds were addicted) had crept down over the windows and doors, was in the process of sealing the door shut forever with its clinging roots; but still the light bulb burned inside . . .

I was afraid that with the miracle of birdsong, it was Grandfather's last night on earth — that the stars and the birds and the forest had granted him one last gift — and so I drove slowly, wanting to remember the taste, smell, and feel of all of it, and to never forget it. But when I stopped the truck he seemed rested, and was in a hurry to get out and go join Father, who was sitting on the porch in the dark listening to one of the spring-training baseball games on the radio. I got out to help him out, but he was already hurrying across the lawn, looking ghostly in the white linen suit he was wearing that day, and he sat down in his chair next to my father without mentioning a word of his birdsong, and I sat down in the grass in front of them and listened to the drone of the game, the sound that was not a sound, and looked up at the stars, at the constellations, at the quarter moon . . . Omar was in his room studying, and after a while we saw the window-cast of his light turn off, and he came out on the porch too and listened to the end of the game with us, a spring training game, a game that did not matter . . .

*

Driving back to college early every Monday morning, up before daylight to make my eight o'clock class. Deer moving through the hill country fog, the familiar white-tailed deer and, increasingly, the larger, more aggressive, herd-forming axis deer, imported from Africa to place on exotic game ranches for the fat boys from the cities to come shoot. The Bankers. Big horns, little penises, I always say. The axis deer slipping through the game ranches' fences, spreading into the countryside. Sometimes I imagine I can feel the earth pause in its rotation, can feel it pause and look at us as if wondering, *Just who the hell do you think you are?*

It occurred to me that if I ever lived to be as old as Grandfather (or even Father), white-tailed deer might be gone from the hill country — an unimaginable thought at first, for there are hundreds of thousands of them, perhaps millions.

In any event, it would not be a thing I wanted to see.

I'd park the truck and run up the steep steps to class. Sit by the window. Chemistry, geology, biology, physics, zoology: I took the classes, read the books, listened to the lectures like Grandfather sipping that tea — drinking it all in, thirsty and drinking it all, until I imagined that my own insides were sparkling with it, all those different stories and that knowledge, which led only further and further into delicious mystery.

*

The next time I was home was in the middle of March — the golden-cheeked warblers had been back a week — and Grandfather had taught himself to speak again: had been keeping it a secret from everyone, waiting for me to return.

The way he had to do it — speak — was by imitating birds' songs — that is, his words had to follow the climbing-and-then-descending pattern of the birds, so that everything he said, he had to sing, sometimes punctuating midsentence with an *ah-ah* as he drew more air, or cast in his mind for the continued melody — but they were words once again, and full sentences, human sentences, and he was back in the world of man again, fully, for better or worse, and the more he practiced, the better he got.

We were picnicking at Mother's grave, Grandfather and I, when a goshawk whistled past us, out and over the cliff, like a thought one has and then forgets immediately.

Grandfather looked up, cleared his throat, and sang,

quavering, his first real words in seven years: "The natural history of Texas is still being sacrificed upon the altar of generalization. *Pay attention,*" he said-sang, and took a swallow of tea, and then another bite of sandwich, as if no time had ever gone by.

Even now, so many days and years later, I remember things that I thought I had forgotten, that I thought were gone forever. I'll call Omar in Philadelphia and tell him. The job is never done — reminding him of his heritage — for it is only us, here on this one piece of land; everything else is being washed away or changing. We are bedrock, however; she wants us to be bedrock, and that requires memory, and storytelling, to those who will someday be the new bedrock . . .

When she was sick — when she was very sick, near the edge — Father caught a four-pound bass, which thrilled her, made her so proud. The excitement — the jolt of that day, the utter pure goodness of it — I'd forgotten it all.

We cooked the big fish's fillets over mesquite. It was a great meal, early autumn, down there by the river, with all of us still alive . . . a perfect day. I'd forgotten that. It must have been hidden in the shadows of grief.

*

Mother taught me to never complain, to never talk about one's troubles. It was not a lesson she ever spoke to me out loud — in the way that I never told Omar she was with us, when I took him to the edges of places, back when we were children. It was just the way she lived that taught me to never complain about my troubles. To never even mention them.

*

I had three boyfriends in college. The first two were trifling and insignificant, only about sex, which wasn't very good anyway — time spent I wish I had back. The third one mattered. He had some of my father's quiet nobility — his single-minded, singularly focused kind of loyalty — and he had my grandfather's wildness, too: that stored passion, and tension — and an opinion, a judgment, on everything he looked at, everything he smelled, tasted, heard, saw, or touched.

He was a big man studying small bugs; his name was Fred Whitehead. I was taking ornithology classes, of course, and that was how we met: he was in one of my bird classes, wanting to know more about the feathered devils that ate his beloved insects.

"Right of capture," I teased him, remembering the Catfish Man's foolish excuse for draining all that clear water, so long ago. But before it was over, what got captured was me. We were both twenty-one, but he was so much smarter — more learned — than I was. He said it was from studying insects (he got angry when I called them bugs). He said that the secrets of life, the mysteries of the universe can be found by those willing to get down on their hands and knees. Even now, I don't know if he was talking about sex. He had an incredible passion for it, just as he did for his . . . insects. I don't know. He had a flaming energy for everything; he seemed to be drawing some energy from the core of the earth, so that he only got stronger in situations that would ultimately wear the rest of us down.

I never saw him yawn; never saw him less than enthusiastic about anything. In the way that I imagined Grandfather's veins and arteries to be filled with gold, copper, and silver, glittering and crystalline, I imagined that Fred seethed with magma: that it flowed through him, around and around, always recirculating. When he came inside me, I thought perhaps it might burn, might alter me, but I wanted it to. When he touched me, I imagined I might be scalded.

Of course I had to show him the ranch.

In the next year that followed, he became like family —
it seemed that we were back up to five. Omar thought Fred
was like some new smart insect-loving brother. Father was
pleased with Fred because I was happy, and probably, too,
because Fred had a real passion in life, a cause and a belief,
despite his youth, that went beyond our romance. It was
part of our romance. It wasn't all physical.

Grandfather kept his distance, but he liked Fred, I could
tell. He saw Fred's energy. He saw Fred's wild heart. I think
Grandfather felt a little conflict within, that Fred had so much
of it, while his, Grandfather's, was finally, slowly fading.

We were finishing our undergrad degrees and would be
going on to A&M in the next year for graduate work. I
wasn't going to specialize . . . was just going to keep taking
classes, getting broader and broader. I wanted to take in as
much as I could hold. Specialized research for me meant
netting and banding birds, and I didn't want any part of
that.

But still, I wanted to know secrets.

What can I say? He enriched our lives. We spent a large
portion of our time that summer on our hands and knees,
as yet another new world opened up for me, and for my
family. Around the dinner table (slabs of venison roast
falling away from the knife; Father carving it, and steam rising from the knife), Fred would tell us stories about insects;
about bombardier beetles that mix defensive chemicals in
their glands to spray their enemies with a liquid whose
temperature is 212 degrees Fahrenheit: boiling.

He was just a boy, but he was fast on his way to becoming a man. He smoked a pipe! After dinner we would go
out on the back porch and watch the dusk, would listen to
the crickets. Whenever Grandfather spoke — often to ask a
question of Fred, for even in his ninetieth year Grandfather
was still interested in learning — birds would swarm us, at-
tracted by the melody of Grandfather's sentences. Fred

would pretend to wince when the bats came out, flitting and swooping after all the insects we couldn't even see.

"Go back to Transylvania," he'd cry out, but I knew he was teasing — he was studying specifically the predator-prey relationships between bats and moths — between the *Myoxis* bat and the *Catocala* moth — and I knew he couldn't love one and not the other. It would be like loving the earth and not the sky; it would be like loving warmth and heat, but not coolness.

Fred told us that the fossil record indicated there was an evolutionary trend toward increasing brain sizes, and that it was probably because of their highly evolved hunting strategies: what he called the rawest, most immediate, demanding challenge of intelligence. I remember how Grandfather hooted and laughed when Fred said that, clapping his hands on his legs, and I think it hurt Fred's feelings, but I could tell Father liked what Fred had said and was thinking about it, and I suspected that Grandfather was, too . . .

Another night, Fred told us that there was some indication that insects in the tropics practice "self-medication" — searching out and ingesting and absorbing secondary compounds that aid in the treatment of insect diseases and injuries, and even cancers, and at the mention of that word we grew quiet, though it was a calm kind of quiet, and I think we all pictured the insects in the night, hurting, creeping through the tropics and searching among the ferns and the rotting logs for their salvation, under the holiness of the stars . . .

When Fred stood up, he blocked out some of the stars. He was a big man: six feet five inches tall. But just a boy. A pipe-smoking boy.

Fred and I would walk down to the creek after dark. The smell of his pipe smoke was like a trail that any predator could follow, but there was only us. We were *solitary*. We bathed in the river. The moonlight welded us to the river in silver. Fred said that some insect copulations lasted up to 136 hours — pushing me through the water, laughing.

We'd wake up on the bank at sunrise some mornings, with great blue herons wading through the mist, spearing frogs. The sunrise red over the summer-velvet hills.

I was afraid he didn't love me enough.

*

The things I put up with for love! I was confused but fascinated by the small changes I found myself making. We'd go out into the woods and test his different hypotheses. Fred believed that avian predators have learned to hunt caterpillars by searching for the slightly chewed edges of a leaf. (He also believed that caterpillars were evolving to move rapidly away from a feeding site, because of this.)

He'd take fingernail clippers and trim up the edges of different plants. We'd hide in camouflage and watch. A bird would pass over, then pause, fluttering — hovering, like the angel of death, before passing on, mystified that there was no caterpillar.

That seemed to me no different from Grandfather calling the birds in for a closer look: just a momentary deception, with a kind of innocence to it.

But Fred was harder. He had that *magma*. By midsummer we were netting some of the birds, trying to learn what they ate, when they ate it, and how much. He never killed a bird, not even a sparrow, as did some other researchers, but still, he *touched* them. I understand now that the reason I let him touch the birds on Prade Ranch was the reason I let him touch me; and that there was no difference. I should have asked the birds about it, but I didn't. I was in love, and had all the grace of an ox running through a cornfield. I wondered if this was how it had been for Mother.

It was delicious. I wanted nothing to do with it, in the classroom, but out in the field, with Fred, it was delicious. I grew stronger; I knitted, healed, mended.

We would fit the larger nestlings, such as those of the

cliff-nesting hawks and ravens, with a neck collar, which allowed the nestling to breathe, but not swallow. A few hours later we'd climb up to the nest and turn the bird upside down and shake out all of the food that the nestling had been unable to swallow — a writhing mass of beetles, wasps, desiccated minnows, berries . . .

We were barbaric, but so close to both mystery and knowledge, and our senses so inflamed with the scent of these things, that we forgot about reverence. We were just hungry — starved.

We were always making love. I think that it was abnormal. I hope that it was.

*

We picked through the pellets and fecal material of owls and turkeys, the birds that roosted in the same place every night and could be counted on to leave us a sample to discover each morning. Using tweezers, we could find fly wings, beetle legs, and ant abdomens. Fred could often identify the ravaged gut-passed remains all the way down to genus and sometimes even species level.

It's so rare to pass near or next to someone so aflame, much less to connect with them: though not impossible. The best fits in nature are achieved of course over long periods of time, through much settling and eroding and uplifting, repositioning . . . but with Fred, the old cliché of falling in love, or swimming in it, was true. To know so much, he loved to listen. I do not think it was my imagination that wherever he touched me, or I touched him, my skin against his and his against mine, was a fit. Not forever, but in that moment, it was always a fit. We were both growing like crazy; growing stronger and feeling the world more deeply each day, and it was like nothing but falling. Our mouths on each other's skin, after swimming. Me listening to him, for a while, and then him listening to me. We could almost hear ourselves growing.

Birds: always we followed birds. He knew so much.

But I taught him things, too; it wasn't all learning, on my part. The brown cowbirds that were taking over the country — the way they'd act as parasites, with a female laying her eggs in a golden-cheeked warbler's nest and then abandoning them: the mother warbler warming and hatching those dull eggs in addition to her own. And when the eggs hatched, because the large cowbirds were more boisterous, they got all the food. The delicate beautiful warbler chicks — an endangered species — languished, then starved to death in their own nest, or were pushed out, or crushed by the clumsy brown cowbird nestlings; and even the mother warbler succumbed then, exhausted by the demands of the gangling cowbird nestlings, just about the time they were ready to take flight.

Fred was delighted by the horrible story.

"The brown ways of the world!" he cried. "They must be avoided!"

"Right," I said. I was thinking *avoid* meant to hole up and make a stand . . . to live a life, the way Mother and Father had. To maintain; to preserve what you believed in. But something bothered me, far inside, and it occurred to me a little later on that to *avoid* in some species meant to flee.

But above the surface, it was all wonderful: it was the most halcyon summer I ever spent. We walked the river in the daytime, talking and watching and listening and holding hands, sitting in the dust, in the cool shade beneath the big oaks, and just listening to the mourning doves. We polished Chubb's Cadillac (ferns and vines growing down into its open carriage), and I lifted the lid to the urn and looked in at the cool blue ashes. I remembered how great and hot the fire had been the day we burned him.

We swam at night like otters, silvery in the moonlight. I have never fit a man so well, nor has a man fit a river so well, nor has water rolled more cleanly, more smoothly, off the bodies of animals, off the curved backs, the round breasts, the oval calves, our round mouths . . . It was all circles, all lunar. I never wanted to come out of the river.

The moon shining on my hair, in my eyes, as I swam. The moon on his shoulders. He looked like a giant, swimming at night like that. Lifting his big arms against the sky. Scooping a handful of stars down with each stroke. Swimming past my mother's grave. Feeling her turn in the rock and watch us go past.

Do I obsess — am I obsessed — with the past of my mother's life? Fred once said it seemed that way to him. But his mother was still living — a thing he loved deeply was still living — he had had enough of her (and, truth be told, then some), while I had not had enough.

I did not get enough. She is still here in the present, but in such thin amounts now, and I am so hungry.

*

The fire that was in Fred: even when we were resting, sometimes sore and chafed, from love — even just lying there, I could feel that he was on fire. He never grew tired. Grandfather was growing more tired each day, and even Father was spending less time out on the land, and was talking about retiring — and sometimes I had the perverse, troubling notion that I had brought a cowbird onto the ranch, that Fred was summoning their old energies away from them.

This was not clear-headed thinking.

I simply did not want to admit the truth of their aging. I was selfish and greedy and I wanted more. I was twenty-two, but wanted to be seven or eight again. If they were horses, I was riding them to the ground with my demands for their love: all of them, Fred included.

I sat with Grandfather and Father and Omar and listened to the ball games: another dead-level .500 season for the Astros.

Larry Dierker. The Red Rooster. Turk Farrell. Jimmy "the Toy Cannon" Wynn. I learned all the names, that late summer, as if they were genus and species, and learned their habits, too: why Lee May couldn't bunt, and when Joe Morgan was likely to steal home.

I believe that Grandfather loved me more because of it. I don't know if that's a good thing or a bad thing to say, but I believe it. I knew that I was losing him, and yet we all had the courage to draw closer, to weave tighter, even all the way into the end.

Fred worked in the study, under the glow of yellow light, like an angel — we could see him in there, through the glass doors — while the rest of us sat or lay on the patio under the sky and the stars. Sometimes Grandfather would reach down, searching for my hand, find it, and squeeze it. *The last bloodline of my mother,* I would think, holding his hand — my last, strongest blood-connection to her — and perhaps he was thinking the same, at those times.

Father and Omar intent upon the game. Grandfather and I intent upon eternity.

*

We'd go out, Fred and I, with lights and netting to try to catch *Myotis* bats, to band them, to study their territorial dynamics and the size of their home ranges in the summer. We'd hang lanterns from the trees every twenty meters along various contours, and count the *Catocala* moths that swarmed each lantern. Omar and I knew them from childhood as "tobacco sphinx" moths, with large round "eyes" on the backs of their wings, which I'd learned were used to startle pursuing birds. A warbler would swoop down just about to grab the resting moth, and the moth would leap into flight: and in that leap, the hidden "eyes" would flash, huge and menacing, and would give the warbler just a split second's pause, and it was that fraction of a moment, that time of suspension, of hover, that sometimes allowed the moth to escape, and to continue living its brief life . . .

But the moths' false wing-eyes didn't help them at night, against *Myotis*. That world — the dark night's goings-on between *Myotis* and *Catocala* — was as close and deep a look into the stars — beyond the stars — as I have ever gotten. It made the predator-prey relationships of mountain lions and deer, or of men chasing women, or of humans chasing some understanding of the afterlife, look simple by comparison.

Everything that is pursued will develop some response appropriate to the pursuit: some shift away from the thing that is chasing it.

But what went on between the bats and the moths while we slept, and what had been going on for millions of years, was as beautiful as the stars themselves.

Like a high-stakes, high-speed game of evolutionary table tennis, the bats have been chasing the moths through the night by echo-locating. The bats emit high-frequency chirps that strike objects and bounce back to the bats' big radar-screen ears. The radar "paints" a picture in the bat's brain instantly: tells it what's out there, what's not, and what the shapes of things are.

Of course those moths that could sense or feel or even hear those invisible, almost inaudible messages — they prospered. They were able to escape, and lived another day to breed, and to pass on those same valuable radar-sensitive genes. *Catocala* and other moths developed over the eons tiny membranous cups along the thorax: receivers tuned specifically to the oncoming bats' radar.

The bats, of course, were not through. Those with slightly different frequencies — higher still, perhaps — were rewarded, evolutionarily speaking; they caught more moths, and prospered. They survived to breed, to pass on those kilohertz genes at a rate exceeding that of their kilohertz relatives.

The moths developed more tympanic membranes, and feathery, pinnated "feelers" — veritable flying gunboats of radar-detection. *Quivering* with sensitivity, with knowledge, picking up every sound, every bit of data, in the world. Of course they can only come out at night.

Some bats, in this game of tag through eternity, cranked it up to over 200 kilohertz; and some of them crapped out, due to the higher caloric demands of maintaining such fire, such intensity.

Other bats, through the eons, worked it down to the lower end of the scale, dropping their signals to around 10 kilohertz. (The average human is conscious of signals up to about 9.8 kilohertz.)

Across the millennia, the moths continued to fly.

Everywhere they went, there were bats waiting for them, looking for them. When the moths first began to flutter their wings, warming up for flight (it's strange to think of moths as having blood), the bats' radar would pick it up, and would be on them in an instant, even before the moth could take flight. Every rustle in the leaves was heard and evaluated by moth and bat alike.

Such were the invisible threads through which Omar and I wandered so blithely as children, our childish laughter echoing amid the bats' invisible calls.

Fred said that he believed moths might move to the daytime, in the next world, the next eon, to escape the bats: but that of course, the bats would follow. Fred worried for the moths (and therefore for the bats) because of how noisy the world was, in all but the quietest places, such as the sandy banks of the Nueces. He had all kinds of recorders and monitors that showed what everyone already knew: that the world was already brimming with noise, excess noise — invisible transmissions, a sizzling roar of it, and he marveled at how the moths and the bats could keep going. Even the sound of a far-off truck going down the highway late at night — one small road cut through the wilderness of scrub, and history — could be heard by both bats and moths, and required a moment's extra energy to pause and evaluate those distant vibrations . . .

There were some bats out there that didn't even need to pick up the moth's movement, in order to find it; these bats could fly right above the tops of leaves, sending out their steady whisper of radar, and could glean in that manner even the frightened, huddled image of a moth clinging motionless to a leaf, hoping the whispering bat will pass it by.

No.

Even up until the final moment of life, bat and moth are linked together forever, through time, and beyond. As a last-gasp evasive maneuver, a fleeing moth will sometimes stop its wingbeats in midflight, thereby ceasing to give off data to the bat's radar. But sometimes the bat will pause, too, so that the moth can't pick up any radar signals — the bat seeming to have disappeared — and for just the briefest of moments they will both hang there, suspended in eternity.

*

Nights in the river, washing off the sweat from the night's labors. The molecules of our sweat being tasted by everything in the river. Our sweat-water lodging in the flesh of the freshwater mussel, being cracked open and eaten by the same raccoon that three nights later would watch Fred and I out in the shallows, double-backed, thrashing like alligators; Fred above me, holding me under the river for a moment (the moon blurry, and Fred again blocking the stars and part of the mountains), or me above Fred, holding him underwater in the shallows, there at the last of it: and pausing, then, both of us pausing, right at the last, for one second, two seconds, for as long as we could.

Three seconds, even four. The river rushing past.

*

It is a gradual kind of strengthening. It takes a long time to see how the losses build you up, rather than strip you down and wear you away. In early September, Fred did not go back to school with me. He had made plans to go on to Belize, to study bats, and to study insects. Bugs. He asked if I'd go, but I was angry that he'd withheld his plans so long before asking — as if unsure I'd pass some test he was conducting. I was angry, and again, for a moment — for long moments — felt as if my growing strength, my growing self, was rocked, knocked off balance, compromised. Weakened; *generalized,* rather than made specific.

I felt tricked by his erratic swerve in flight: all this talk of *Belize,* a week before we were set to go back to school.

It made me think he was hoping I'd say no, was why he'd waited so long; as if he thought he could move faster without me.

It made me think he loved the bugs more than he did me and my family.

"Thirty *million* unnamed species," he said. "Fifty-two species of bats! It'll be *great!* Beaches, bananas, mangoes, guavas . . ."

Grandfather just sitting there on the porch in his rocking chair, watching. The sound of his heavy breathing. Watching.

*

There was one more, after that — one more man of significance, I mean, after Fred — though in the end that man melted before my river-memories of Fred. I'd gotten my doctorate degree, and was going to take a job teaching. The schooling hadn't been easy: so much hoop-jumping bullshit in the world of science, and no more sacred awe. That came only on the weekends, when I could get back to the ranch. (A four-hour drive from College Station, each way.)

Grandfather was ninety-six. Omar was graduating from Brown, and would be coming back to law school at UT. It was a long trip now for Grandfather to walk, even from the back porch to Chubb's old vined-over stone house, and though Grandfather could still continue past there and on a good day make it all the way down to the river and the gazebo, he couldn't make it back up the steps. A wheelchair wouldn't work over all the rocks and sticks, so we hauled him around in the wheelbarrow when there was something we wanted him to see or somewhere he wanted to go. But mostly he just sat on the back porch and watched the hummingbirds come to the feeders, amazed by their energy.

Father had bought a milk cow and five baby feeder calves, and had taken to raising a few for market each year, mostly for something to do. Cattle on the Prade Ranch! I had to laugh. Grandfather couldn't stand them, bent down and got pebbles and threw them at the calves, said they would wander through the brush and step on the quail eggs and knock the vireo nestlings from their nests and erode the mountains into the river so that it would all be washed out to the sea, all, and in our lifetime, but Father just chuckled and fed the cows more corn out of his hand and said that they never left the yard . . .

In four more years, after Grandfather died, Father would move to Fredericksburg and start a garden: not yet tired of living, but tired, I knew, of wondering what he had missed.

The only other man I was ever to bring out to Prade Ranch was an ex-professor of mine named Stan. He was such a non-item that Grandfather laughed when he saw him. Stan was studying immature bald eagles, and seemed not to worship or be struck dumb by the flying chips of color, the bright songbirds, that came near Grandfather every time he spoke.

"A professor, eh?" Grandfather said, his old eyes laughing — laughing at Stan, and at my embarrassment, for he knew somehow that I wouldn't be with Stan very long. It was during my brief seemingly sophisticated phase: with all the academia in my head, it seemed I should do something with it. Go to cocktail parties. Spend time with boring and overserious people, instead of being in the church of the wild.

I thought of Fred. He'd married some Brazilian bombshell and was living in the foothills of the Andes. He had three children, all girls.

"Yes," Stan said, "a professor." He nodded his head slightly, believing, I think, that the old man was honored that a real professor was on the property — *that's probably a first*, I could see Stan thinking — and Grandfather guffawed until his eyes watered, and I had to nudge him with my foot and give him a fierce look, which made him laugh harder and made him pound the end of his cane against the back porch tiles.

"The natural history of Texas is being sacrificed upon the altar of generalization!" Grandfather cried, as Stan and I were heading down to the river — black-capped vireos rushed in to the sound of Grandfather's voice — and Stan turned and looked back at Grandfather oddly for a moment, wondering, I'm sure, where the hell *that* had come from. I heard Grandfather add, under his breath, "Put *that* in your pipe and smoke it," though Stan did not smoke a pipe, and I do not think he heard him . . .

*

We took a canoe down the river, to watch the eagles. Stan couldn't swim. He had a little black box with him that used GPS, the Global Positioning System, to show him, via satellite imagery, exactly where he was on the map at any given time, right down to the last twenty-foot USGS contour. We canoed past Chubb's viney, sodden Cadillac, with all the old sun-bleached plastic flowers in the seat, and he looked at that oddly too, but had no questions: looked back up at the sky, scanning for eagles, which he kept calling the *i.s.*'s, for indicator species.

I'd heard it all before, a million times before in school, but it seemed a little wearisome, and a little sacrilegious, to be hearing it out in the woods, on the river itself. I was in the stern, paddling, playing the game I'd played as a child, trying to follow the old wagon ruts underwater. There was a stiff cross-breeze, and I kept having to alter my strokes to stay on track.

The ruts drifted beneath us. A large soft-shelled turtle swam below the canoe. The threatened Midland species, genus *Trionyx*, I thought, though I couldn't remember the species or subspecies, and didn't really care. I could look it up in the book later, I thought.

It was a fine spring day, mild and breezy. The warblers and hummers had been back for three weeks. Wildflowers would be blossoming in the hills any day. Baseball season was starting. I thought of how timeless the river was.

Up in the bow, Stan was tuning his little black box, and folding and refolding his topo map to see exactly where he was. He was blathering about gap analysis and DEMs, and I started to laugh.

We were coming up on Mother's spot, and suddenly I didn't want to go any farther. I put the paddle in the water and braced, still laughing, and backstroked. I ferried us over to the shore, just before we would have rounded the bend.

"What?" Stan asked. "What's so funny? Where are we going?" he asked; the wind carrying the tinkling of his words down the river.

*

That night at supper we had a big venison ham that Father had been mesquite-smoking and marinating down at the gazebo all day. It was a deer he'd shot last year, a huge buck he'd rattled right into within ten yards: an old deer, well past his prime. Father was more proud of that big old deer than any other he'd ever hunted.

I'd forgotten to tell them Stan was a vegetarian.

"You eat this meat," I whispered to him. "I want you to say a prayer at the table thanking the land and my father for this meat and then I want you to eat it or I am going to shove it down your throat. *You eat this meat,*" I hissed. "It's good for you."

He ate it, eyes watering. It nearly made him sick, but he ate it, and said it was good. Said the blessing, too.

That evening, before the baseball game, Grandfather went back in his room. He was gone a good while, and I thought he'd gone back there to take a nap, but when I went in to check on him he was bent over, rustling around in his cedar chest.

He straightened up when I came in, and handed me a sheaf of old papers.

"To show your professor," he said. He handed the old parchment (wrapped in ancient cardboard with a strip of leather fastening it) and shrugged, as if it were just old paper. "And for you to look at, if you want. I was saving them for your mother. Watching that professor gag down that hindquarter reminded me of them." He shrugged again. "They're old letters from this fellow Chubb I used to know," he sang, almost in a whisper, and I imagined that the birds, if they could hear him, rustled in their sleep, on their roosts: his words entering their dreams, calling to them. "Fella's name was Homer Young. He saw things we never got to see."

We took the old parchment back into the dining room. Outside, the fireflies were just beginning to blink. It was lonely, without Omar in the house. We were down to just three of us.

The first letter was from a trip Homer Young had made a few counties to the west, looking for work as a school teacher. It was dated February 17, 1902.

> *Dear Chubb and Frank,*
>
> *Landlord Holman, of the Monahan Hotel, who is an old-timer here, informs me that the last buffalo in this region was killed in the winter of 1885 by a professional hunter, George Fischer, who is credited with having killed more buffalo than any other man in Texas. People said they didn't like this arid country and were not found hereabouts, but in the fall and summer of 1884, Fischer killed several over near the southeast corner of New Mexico, and finally, in January 1885, while riding to Midland, came up with the last two remaining animals, a cow and a calf, near a water hole. Fischer shot the cow and roped the calf, which he finally turned over to Mr. C. C. Winn, of Fort Worth, who eventually had it killed for a large barbecue. Said the meat was reported as "tasty."*

The twilight deepened. Grandfather stared at the old paper a long time. I was furious that mother wasn't here to see it, to hear it: and strangely upset with Grandfather, too, that he'd forgotten to share it with her.

It still seemed as if she had just gone away for a little while. After all this time, it still seemed like she would be coming back, and that we could tell her about it then.

I saw that Grandfather was crying without sound: his eyes glistening, and his cheeks wet. A tear spackling the old paper.

He shuffled listlessly through the papers. Even Stan, who'd stepped in quietly, was paying attention.

"Here's another one," Grandfather sang. "From Fredericksburg Hotel, March 20, 1905."

Yours of 15th in hand. In regard to the jaguar, we killed him Thursday night, September 3. Big moon. I will give you some of the particulars. Old Mr. Brooks came to go hunting with me that night. I had a boy staying with me by the name of John Dallas Thompson. We took supper at my home and then started for the mountains, three miles, and treed him in a small Spanish oak. Old Mr. Brooks shot him in the body with a Colt .45. He fell out of the tree and the hounds ran him about half a mile and bayed him. Old Mr. Brooks had lost his bullets in the chase so I stayed with him while Brooks and the boy, John Dallas, went back to Willow City after more guns and ammunition. I was sorry we had caught up with him and sorry we had shot at him and tried to make him leave the tree, but he wouldn't.

In about an hour and a half Brooks and Thompson came back and brought several men with them, so then the fight commenced. We had to ride into the shinnery and drive him out, and we got him killed just at twelve o'clock that night. We commenced the fight with ten hounds, but when we got him killed there were three dogs with him, and one of them wounded. He killed one dog and very nearly killed several others, causing them to run home. He also got hold of Howard Burrier's horse and bit it so bad it died from the wounds.

The jaguar measured 7½ feet from tip to tip, 36 inches around chest, 26 inches around head, 21 inches around forearm, 9¼ inches across the bottom of the foot. Weight, 140 pounds.

In regard to how the jaguar came there, my idea is that it made its way up the San Saba River and across the Colorado and up toward Gillespie County. I took particular note of the country around Fredericksburg and in that part where the animal was killed it is rough with rocky ridges which they call "mountains," running parallel with the creeks and rivers, with uneven valley lands between the

streams and the mountains. There is no tall timber, but the
entire country is covered with a thick brush, or chaparral,
consisting chiefly of shin oak thickets known as the "shin-
nery"; also sumac thickets and Spanish oak clumps with
live oaks along the creeks.

Grandfather closed his eyes when he had finished reading, and appeared to be asleep, but then he opened his eyes
and looked straight at me with eyes so clear that I knew he
was seeing everything: not just me, and not just my mother,
thirty years ago, but into the future, too — into the very
near future.

I took the dishes in, Stan and I cleaned them, and then
we all went out onto the porch to pick up the baseball
game. It was windy, and it was hard finding the signal: the
voice sounded very small and far away, and kept drifting in
and out, almost a whisper.

That night in bed with Stan I listened to the wind rock
the tin roof of the house. He was warm, and I moved in
closer against him, even as in my mind I moved farther
away. So far away. All the way back to the northeast corner.

We were down to three of us, and then we would be
down to two, and then to one. And then there would just
be the land. This thought comforted me, and I fell asleep
listening to the wind rock us to sleep.

*

Grandfather died a few days after his hundredth birthday.
Both Father and I were there at the end, in the room where
I'd been born, forty-four years ago. It was not unlike that
day, with sunlight streaming through the windows, and
hummingbirds hovering outside, iridescent sun-glittering
flashes of jewels. A dove was calling, back in the cool shade.
Grandfather's hand was cool, as cool as the river. He tried
to sit up to look out at the sunlight.

"Sycamores grow by running water," he sang, "cotton-woods by still water," and then he died, and I felt a century slip away.

*

I live here on the Prade Ranch alone — already years be-yond the age my mother was when she returned to the ranch — to the particular elements of the earth: soil, water, carbon, sky. You can rot or you can burn but either way, if you're lucky, a place will shape and cut and bend you, will strengthen you and weaken you. You trade your life for the privilege of this experience — the joy of a place, the joy of blood family; the joy of knowledge gotten by listening and observing.

For most of us, we get stronger slowly, and then get weaker slowly, with our cycles sometimes in synchrony with the land's health, though other times independent of its larger cycles. We watch and listen and notice as the land, the place — *life* — begins to summon its due from us. It's so subtle . . . a trace of energy departing here, a trace of impulse missing there. You find yourself as you have always been, square in the middle of the metamorphosis, constantly living and dying: becoming weaker in your strength, finally. Perhaps you notice the soil, the rocks, or the river, taking back some of that which it has loaned to you; or perhaps you see the regeneration occurring in your daughter, if you have one, as she walks around, growing stronger. And you feel for the first time a sweet absence . . .

I remember a game Omar and I used to play, when we were small. Scorpions would glow in the dark, after we'd loaded them up with light by shining our flashlight on them. Not every scorpion would glow like this, but some would — about one in a hundred, maybe one in a thousand. We'd lift up rocks, under the moonlight, and shine our lights on the scorpions' backs, looking for such a specimen. And then when we'd find one, we'd fill him with the light from our flashlights, then shut the lights off and follow him, glowing in the dark, across the caliche streambeds, across the slick rock, and across the hills, following him until the glimmer faded, and there was only silence.